LOCAL AUTHOR

CURLEY, Daniel

Love in the winter: stories. Urbana,
Univ. of Illinois Pr. [c1976]
118p. (Illinois short fiction) (An
Illini book)

I. tc.

Love in the Winter

ILLINOIS SHORT FICTION

Love in the Winter

Stories by Daniel Curley

UNIVERSITY OF ILLINOIS PRESS
Urbana   Chicago   London

fic.

"The Great Day," *Accent*, Fall, 1952.
"Love in the Winter," *Colorado Quarterly*, Winter, 1964.
"Why I Play Rugby," *University Review*, Summer, 1971.
"Who, What, When, Where—Why?" *New Letters*, Spring, 1972.
"Perhaps Love," *New Letters*, Spring, 1972.
"A View of the Mountains," *Mississippi Review*, vol. 1, no. 2, 1972.
"What Rough Beast?" *Massachusetts Review*, Spring, 1973.
"The Eclipse," *Hudson Review*, Summer, 1973.
"Power Line," *Epoch*, Spring, 1974.
"In Northumberland Once," *Massachusetts Review*, Summer, 1974.

Library of Congress Cataloging in Publication Data

Curley, Daniel.
    Love in the winter.

    (Illinois short fiction)
    CONTENTS: Love in the winter.—Who, what, when,
where, why?—The great day.   [etc.]

    I.   Title.
PZ4. C974Lo   [PS3553.U65]   813'.5'4   76-7541
ISBN 0-252-00551-1
ISBN 0-252-00578-3 pbk.

Contents

Love in the Winter

"Look," Ross Taylor said, when at last Grace Martin was really in his car, "instead of dropping off at the station, why don't you ride overland with me as far as Albany or Syracuse and take your train on from there?" He hesitated, appalled at the traps opening out of the simplest words. "The Berkshires will be worth seeing in all this snow, the Mohawk Trail, the Taconic Trail and all," he concluded lamely. He was glad to have got out of that corner without basing his appeal on some assumption either of his overwhelming personal magnetism or of his pathetic loneliness. (It will make the trip more pleasant for you/for me/for both of us.)

"I was hoping you'd say something like that," Grace said. Taylor had been writing the dialogue in his head for the past three days, ever since they agreed it would be convenient for Grace to drive to the station with him when he left to go back to Chicago. He had written that very speech for her, in fact, but now that he actually heard her speaking it, he felt like a vast jellyfish from his throat to his hips.

There was a lot he was supposed to say now, but he forgot it all. "Good," he said, "good." Fortunately Grace had a great many things to say about sending a telegram to excuse her change of plans, and he had to make a great many replies that didn't need thinking about.

So shaken was he, however, by the success of his opening move and even more by his audacity in making it at all that he found himself unable to concentrate on the next moves in his campaign. His mind jumped from one irrelevancy to another, but kept returning to simple wonder that she was there at all.

Why, four days ago, before he had even met her, he despised her. It wasn't enough that she was to be in the Harrises' guest room so that he would have to bed down in the study. No indeed, she had to be a dean of women on top of that, and Taylor was full of the traditional academic contempt for administrators. Of course he hadn't had much to do with deans of women in recent years, but he remembered the breed well from his days as a young instructor jumping from hick school to hick school. Probably the one where she was dean was just like the lot of them.

His first look at her had shaken him, but he steadied himself while he took off his coat and greeted the Harrises, watching her all the while. She didn't look like a dean of women. That was hard to forgive. In fact, she didn't look like an old school chum of Jean Harris. Obviously, as a spinster dean she had been able to take care of herself. He compared her quickly with Jean, who was iron gray and almost a nervous wreck, and with his own wife, who was now built like the Hollywood version of a Russian lady truck driver. As he moved closer, he saw that she had black hair and light eyes, a combination that never failed to move him profoundly. He was profoundly moved and despised her the more bitterly for it.

By the time the house had quieted down, however, and he lay on the couch in the study (it was really very comfortable) enjoying a last cigarette, he had so far changed his mind that he was wondering what would happen if tomorrow he found an opportunity to make her one of the vile proposals that had been running through his mind all evening from the very moment they shook hands and their eyes met and she opened with something other than the standard dean of women's gambit: "We'll get along fine—after all we're in the same game." He had been ready for that, but it didn't come, and he soon realized that she was quite incapable of it. At the same time, she was only politely interested in how his paper had gone at the Modern Languages convention that day and didn't pretend ever to have heard of the Finnesburh Fragment or any problems connected with it. She didn't even pretend to be interested. All this without leaving the least doubt that she was very much interested in him.

Before he finally fell asleep that night, he even went so far as to wonder what would happen if he had the courage then and there to pad on bare feet through the dark house and quietly try the knob of the guest room door. He told himself that he read too many dirty books. He reminded himself of the sanctity of his host's house. He reminded himself of his wife and children. He assured himself that he wasn't that kind of man. In short, he did nothing, neither that night nor the two following nights.

Each day he assured himself that he would make a move if he again caught that look that seemed to enter him like an enormous jolt of neat whiskey and explode into fire inside him. Each day he caught the look but did nothing. Well, not exactly nothing. He did check train and plane schedules and find that if she would agree to give up going by way of New York for the sake of seeing some old friends for a few hours between trains, and if she would agree to drive with him as far as Albany, they could manage a night in Albany if she would agree to that. He had it all worked out, but he didn't believe for a minute that he would ever be able to ask her.

And now it was done. They were actually driving together through the snow across Massachusetts. Of course there were still uncertainties, but if he was careful everything would lead where he wanted to go. His heart pounded at the mere idea of closing a hotel room door on himself and a strange woman. Unfortunately he could see only as far as that gesture, and he had no idea what came next. It was like a honeymoon, of course, but he had never had a honeymoon. How do people get over those first minutes alone? How long or how short is it before you can say, For God's sake, let's get to bed? Probably, since they would both know why they were there, it would work out all right, but in his imagination he remained all night with his hand on the doorknob.

With his wife he had never had to confront that problem. It had already been taken care of before they were even introduced. They had waked up in bed together after a party, very publicly compromised. In fact, it was their host's pounding on the bedroom door that awoke them. Their host and hostess had not slept well on the living room couches and were not disposed to let anyone else sleep, especially in their own bed, especially people who, no matter what éclat they had given the party, had caused all kinds of complications by locking themselves in with all the hats and coats.

During the following week, Taylor was at some pains to find out the name of the girl—his host and hostess wouldn't speak to him. But when he found her, she wouldn't speak to him either. At last she consented to a meeting in a public place. One meeting led to another. Taylor began with apology and ended with the offer of his sacred treasure. She hesitated, and Taylor's fate hung in the balance for weeks—why, she scarcely knew him—and all the while they continued to see each other in public places. Taylor was secretly horrified at what had happened, and at the same time he was secretly delighted.

In later years, however, the emotion that drove out all others was regret: regret that he had found the girl and that she had married him, thereby causing him to lose a precious secret that he might otherwise have held with warm pleasure and consolation in marriage with someone else; and regret that all the people who had been at the party had long ago drifted out of his life and there was now no one left to keep the legend alive.

Today with Grace was going to be more like the beginning of a honeymoon, for all day there would be anticipation while they drove together intimately through the snow. The words "A Night of Love" hung in the air before him as solid as if cut out of stone, as brilliant as if floodlighted on a marquee.

The snow continued to fall all day, but the roads were still good. The car was heavy, and the snow treads gave good traction even in the Berkshires. However, everything was taking longer than Taylor had planned. Never had one of those tiny New England states seemed so endless, and it was well after two o'clock when they finally stopped for lunch in Williamstown. They would get into Albany early enough, but the sense of leisure was being eaten away, and a familiar tension was building up in the back of Taylor's neck.

As soon as they left Williamstown and began climbing the Taconic Trail, Taylor began to be on the lookout for the state line.

Not the least of the incidental pleasures of the day was the knowledge that he would be violating the Mann Act. The very thought that he—Ross Taylor, for God's sake—was transporting a woman across a state line for immoral purposes in full defiance of the Federal Government and the Seventh Commandment, at the risk of his loving wife, his gratifying children, his flourishing career—that terrible thought was delicious indeed.

He knew they must be getting close to the line, and he was preparing a light speech about the Mann Act to give himself yet another *frisson* when she said suddenly, "What's that up ahead?"

Engrossed in his fantasy, he had been aware only of the immediate problems of driving, but now he saw two cars standing in the road just about where he imagined the line to be. He automatically slowed and shifted down into second so as not to lose his traction on the hill. "Looks like an accident," he said.

"Oh I hope not," she said. "I hope no one's hurt."

By then they were close enough to see better. "No," he said, "it's not an accident. The New York plows haven't come this far, and those cars are stuck."

"Do you think we could help them?" she said.

"Not likely," he said. "I'm going to go on through, and we can leave word for the state police at the first town we come to."

"Do you think we should stop and say we'll send help?"

His neck was now so stiff he didn't expect ever to be able to move his head again. "I don't want to lose my momentum," he said, making an effort to control his temper. After all she wasn't his wife even if she did sound like a wife the way she was asking the questions he had resolved not to think about. He made a further effort. "The top of the trail is just beyond the state line. You can see it from here. Up at that bend where the wind has swept the road bare. It's downhill from there. I think we'll be all right."

"I'm sure we will."

Just hearing that was almost reward enough in itself. He had forgotten—if he ever knew—how good it is for a man to hear such things. However, he was by no means sure himself that they would get through, but he knew that their schedule was already so badly out of order that it couldn't stand much more delay.

"We'll be all right," he said again as they left behind the plowed roads and entered the rutted snow of New York State.

She said, "My mother always maintained she could tell the minute she left Massachusetts, but I never believed it until now."

He laughed because just then he was forging past the first of the stuck cars. It was a Model A and was sitting squarely on the road. It hadn't got far, and he would have thought it could be backed out without much trouble. He glanced at the driver, an old woman in a fur coat and fur cap, who smiled at him and waved him on and blew her horn in encouragement as he went past.

The second car was almost at right angles to the road with its rear end against the snow bank to the left. There was room for him to pass, but he was afraid for a minute his wheels were going to start to spin on him as he edged over off the crown of the road, but he shifted down into first and kept going.

Both his shoulders ached now, but he was very conscious of his skill in keeping his wheels under him. "It won't be long now," he said, thinking as he said it only of getting over the mountain but realizing at once that it might be considered a crude allusion. He hoped she knew he couldn't do a thing like that—yes, or she wouldn't be with him at all. Then he hit a snow drift. The car would move neither forward nor back with all his skill. "I guess that's it," he said, and immediately the tension began to be less. "We can be warm here a long time with the heater, and we have the radio if we get bored with each other's company." He flicked the radio on to demonstrate.

"Bored already?" she said.

"Nothing but football," he grunted. Being a husband for twenty years had at least taught him some arts of silence.

"Let's listen to a game for a little," she said. "I don't really feel it's New Year's unless I hear a touchdown or two."

"Any preference?"

"Rose Bowl, of course," she said. "It's more like Santa Claus." She was disappointed, however, to find that Alabama was being beaten in the Rose Bowl. "They're supposed to win," she said. "The Rose Bowl jinx."

They listened for what seemed to him like a long time. Each time he leaned forward to adjust the radio, he was conscious of her nearness, each time he lit her cigarette. The football game did not exist for him. During a time out she said, "Do you think using the radio like this will run down the battery too much?"

"No, it's all right." He knew he had been a little curt—his wife would have noticed it anyway—so he added with some effort, "Running the motor like this is keeping the battery up." He wasn't sure about that, but he hoped so anyway.

"Perhaps we shouldn't be running the motor so much."

"There's plenty of gas," he said. "I filled it at Williamstown."

"I mean, how about carbon monoxide and all that? I don't think the school would care to have its dean of women found in a parked car on a lonely mountain road."

"It would teach the girls always to be sure a window is open a bit. You'd be a martyr for education."

She laughed and he felt repaid for the effort, which had been considerable.

"Besides," she said, "it's not really so lonely, not with them." She gestured toward the other cars, but Taylor knew it was the nearer she meant, about twenty yards back down the slope. That car and Taylor's car were both slewed across the highway so that they were at right angles to each other. A man and a woman sat stiffly on the front seat staring through the windshield as if Taylor's car were something in a movie.

If it had not been for those spectators, Taylor would have felt obliged to consider whether this was the time to make his pass. But even so, the light was beginning to fail. The tension in his shoulders was returning. He peered up and down the trail to see if any help was in sight. "Here comes more company," he said, "and by the looks of things he won't get far."

The car he was watching made a fast run up to the unplowed road and plunged in without slackening speed. "I hope he doesn't chew us up, bulling around like that." The car got past the Model A without trouble, but immediately afterward it began to slew so that to get past the second car it had to slow down noticeably. Once it was past, the driver tramped on the gas, and his wheels began to spin. Very shortly he was squarely across the road just behind Taylor's car.

"Well," Taylor said, "this is more like it. I saw that car being worked on where we stopped for gas in Williamstown. Some college boys on their way back to school rammed a bus and smashed in their grill and radiator—Alabama, too, by the way. It looks like a bad day for Alabama all around. But now there'll be plenty of manpower to help get us out of here—according to the mechanic there are supposed to be six of them."

"You aren't going to do anything rash, are you?" Grace said.

"Good lord," he said. "Rash? What do you mean?" He would have known very well what his wife meant, and he was more than a little dismayed by the intimation that even if he was only borrowed for the night he was to be maintained in good condition.

Before she had a chance to answer, the car was surrounded by boys. Taylor rolled down the window to speak to them. "Good afternoon, sir," the nearest boy said. "We thought we'd get organized and get all four cars out of here. We'll start with the first car down the hill. That will give us a better chance to horse the others around as we come down, right? Are you with us?"

"Right," Taylor said and began to roll up his window.

"Just a minute," Grace said. She leaned across Taylor to speak out the window. The boys crowded around for a good look at her. "What my husband means," she said—Taylor was struck dumb and motionless at that, and she was leaning negligently on his knee besides, her hair brushing his cheek. "What he means is that he's with you in spirit, but the fact is that he's ruptured and can't do that sort of work no matter how much he'd like to. You see how it is."

"Sure," said one of the boys who had not spoken before.

"That's tough," said another.

"Of course," said the one who had been spokesman and whom Taylor had privately labeled Fraternity President. "Can we count on you to drive, sir, if we need you, that is, while the rest of us push?"

"Absolutely," Grace said, quickly sensing that Taylor wasn't going to reply. Taylor, in fact, had not heard the question. He was no longer aware even that he was being smothered by her perfume, her hair, her soft weight against him, a death which he had been contemplating with delight all day up to that very moment.

He was not aware of his surroundings even when she had rolled up the window and withdrawn. "I'm sorry," she said, touching his sleeve.

"That's all right," he said automatically. He also performed the gesture of patting her hand without having to return to the full unpleasantness of consciousness.

"I didn't want to do that," she said. "I knew it would hurt you—as if you needed to prove anything to those kids—"

"No, it's really all right, Betty," he said, making an effort to reassure her and turning toward her. He felt as if he had run into something in the dark when he saw that it was not actually his wife who was reading his wife's lines. He remembered vividly that he had called her by his wife's name. "That's done it," he said.

"What?" she said.

"On top of everything else, calling you by the wrong name."

"Don't think about it," she said. "In fact under the circumstances it might even be a sort of compliment, but I really don't mind anyway. I'm the one really who owes you apologies."

"No, no," he said. He had withdrawn from her as far as possible. "You did absolutely the right thing. I shouldn't have forced you to do it. It was nothing but my vanity. You were right about that."

"And men laugh at women for dressing to please other women," she said. He could tell that she would have laughed if he had been able to give her the least encouragement. "What does a thing like that matter?"

This succeeded in diverting his attention but probably not as she had intended to divert it. He wanted to ask her how she knew about that old rupture although he was aware there was only one way she could have heard of it. The whole question of what women talk about among themselves came up before him, and bitterly he faked a quotation he couldn't quite remember. "I had a gossip," he said, "and one friend more/That if my husband had but pissed against a wall/I must have run to tell them of it all."

"Well," she said, "is *that* the Finnesburh Fragment?"

"No," he said, "it's the Wife of Bath, who knew more about men and women than anybody. She had five husbands, you know."

"It's not very nice to have anybody know—" She broke off in some confusion. "When things begin to go wrong," she said, "they just go wrong."

"No," he said, "it will still be all right. Why, they've got one car out already and are working on the next. We'll be back in Williamstown in an hour, and if we have to stay there, why then we stay there, and leave for Albany very early in the morning." He knew he wasn't being very realistic about it because the Model A had been no trouble at all, but now, with the second car, the boys were already floundering in the snow and showing signs of exhaustion.

"We'll see," she said. "I'd rather be in Albany tonight if possible though."

"We'll do it barring an act of God," he said.

It was very nearly dark when the boys came back to Taylor's car. "Would you mind," the Fraternity President said, "if we get into your car to rest awhile before we tackle our own car? We don't have a heater."

"By all means," Taylor said, "and, look, I've got some whiskey in the trunk. Let me get it."

"We wouldn't say no," said one of the boys who had already climbed into the back seat.

The moment Taylor stuck his head out the door, the wind whipped off his hat. Before anyone could move a step, the hat had sailed down the road, over the snow bank, and out across the valley. Taylor watched it go until it disappeared far below in the snow and dark. "Beautiful," he said. "The most pleasure I've ever had from any hat I've ever owned." His ears felt cold at once, but he thought he was behaving very well. Then he realized that none of the boys had been wearing hats all the while. "Let me get the whiskey," he said.

When he came back with the whiskey, he found the doors closed and the car full. The Rose Bowl game was on again. The Fraternity President was sitting at the wheel. "I thought," the President said, "that you might not mind holding your wife on your lap for a while."

"Oh," Taylor said, "no, of course not."

"Well, I mind," Grace said. "An old married woman like me doesn't get as many chances as all that to sit on young men's laps. You might have asked me. And so, dear, with your permission—"

"Or without it, I dare say," Taylor say bitterly.

"Never," she said, laughing. "Now if this gentleman will be so kind as to accommodate me—" She indicated the boy next to her on the seat.

"Speak up, clown," the Fraternity President said.

"Sure," the boy said.

"He says he is honored, madam," the President said.

"Tell him thank you," she said.

"OK," the President said.

"OK," the boy said.

"He says he is quite at your convenience."

She slid onto the boy's lap and the President slid from behind the wheel and Taylor got in out of the cold. He passed Grace the full bottle, out of courtesy, of course, but at the same time he knew he would be able to tell if she was cheating on the drink. Part of his pleasure had been based on the idea of plying her with drink. In fact, that was almost as good as the Mann Act.

She took the bottle and punished it like a man and passed it on, neglecting even the delicacy of a cough and a goddamn, to the boy on whose lap she was sitting. His face had become suddenly very red against the darkness of her coat, and when he drank, he choked and the tears stood in his eyes. He did not omit the goddamn.

The President did not drink but passed the bottle into the back seat, and when it came to him again, he urged it on Taylor as if the bottle had been his own. Taylor felt a stab of irritation and very nearly said, Goddamn it, it's *my* whiskey. But he felt ultimately that he was obliged to demonstrate—if only to himself—the superiority of his manners. He allowed the President to drink last.

"Go, Alabama," the President said as he raised the bottle on high.

"Go, Jinx," the others chorused as if they had been drilled to it.

"It's not too late," the President said. He drank. It was, in fact, much too late. Even Taylor knew it, and he never paid attention to such things as football.

"They're our boys," the others said chorally.

As the second round of drinks began, Grace gave the "Go, Alabama," and was applauded. She asked to be taught an Alabama song and learned with unconvincing difficulty a song that seemed to be mostly about corn likker and arson. At least Taylor was unconvinced although the boys were enchanted.

"Let's go, men," the President shouted, and in very short order, Taylor and Grace were alone in the car while the boys bounded through the snow yelling, "Go, go, go."

"Confess now," Taylor said. "You knew that song."

"Of course," she said. "Even my sweet little freshmen know it. They think it's very daring. We encourage them to think so."

"Apparently the boys are encouraged to think so too," he said, "but I had never heard it."

"Reaily?" she said. "From the way you were trying to catch my eye, I thought maybe that song was the Finnesburh Fragment."

"Now that you mention it, it is very Anglo-Saxon in mood—a getting drunk, boasting, burning down the mead hall sort of thing."

"Then what were you trying to catch my eye about?"

Taylor had to grope for a moment back to the time when all the boys were in the car. Once they were gone he had forgotten all the irritation they had caused. It infuriated him now that he was unable to cherish a manly anger, and he said with rather more heat than he intended, "I thought you were being pretty hard on the kid under you."

"*I* was being hard on *him?*" she said. "That's a laugh."

"You couldn't see his face," Taylor said. "He was embarrassed. He was very uncomfortable."

"I didn't have to see his face. He was enjoying it all right."

"Christ," Taylor said, "the famous feminine intuition never knows a goddamn thing about what a man enjoys or when or how he enjoys it."

"Well, I'll tell you something," she said. "The famous feminine intuition can tell in a minute who was really being given a hard time."

"Me?" Taylor said. "Don't make me laugh. What's it to me if you want to act like a giddy freshman on her first football week-end?"

"I don't know what it is to you, but you sure are making it something."

"Look here," Taylor said. He could have gone on as far as "if you think for one minute that," hoping for some inspiration before he ran out of words, but he was saved by shouts from the boys, who were having some trouble with their own car.

Their car was stopped farther down the slope now and backed into the snow bank. The boys were crowding around the back of the car and looking at something that was hidden from Taylor's car. "It looks as if they have hit something," Taylor said.

"Perhaps someone is hurt," Grace said. One of the boys was already floundering up toward them, and Taylor and Grace were both out of the car waiting when he got there.

"Let me have the whiskey," he panted. Taylor turned to get it. "An accident."

"I'll take it down," Grace said. "I know first aid. Is he badly hurt?"

"Don't know," the boy called back over his shoulder as he ran ahead of them down the trail.

They found that the car had pushed one of the boys into the snow bank and held him there so that he couldn't even move his arms.

"Are you in pain?" Grace asked. The boy, who was obviously terrified, shook his head. Grace tried to pass him the bottle but couldn't reach him.

"Here," one of the boys said. He took the bottle and got into the car and, leaning out the window, held it for the imprisoned boy to drink. He drank as if he was very thirsty, and he did not cough and only added goddamn as an unconvincing afterthought.

"That's the spirit," Grace said.

"Can't you move the car away enough to get him out?" Taylor said.

"We don't know where his legs are," the President said. "We're afraid to spin the wheels."

"Quite," Taylor said to his own surprise, and he lost track of things for a minute until he realized that Americans he knew didn't get into spots like this, but Englishmen were always doing it in novels and movies.

"We're afraid he may be broken up already," the President said in a lowered voice, "but we don't want to upset him more than he is already."

"Just right," Grace said. "How're you feeling, boy?" she called.

The boy in the snow smiled wanly. One of the others called, "Old Horse is resting. He'll take a deep breath in a minute and move it away with his chest." The others laughed very loudly.

"All right," the President said. "Up on the snow bank and let's dig him out."

In ten minutes they had the boy out and were helping him to stand in the road. They were examining him as if he were something they had just unpacked from a crate that had arrived in bad condition. They moved his arms and legs and watched his face for signs of pain. There seemed to be nothing wrong with him although he could scarcely stand and didn't respond to any questions.

"Old Horse is just tired," the President said. Then, in a lower voice but still loud enough for the boy to hear, he said, "He's been working more than any two of the rest."

"I'll take him up to our car and get him warm," Grace said. "Come along, Horse." She took the boy's arm to lead him away, but he shook off her hand and began to follow the car, which the other boys were moving down the trail back into Massachusetts.

"I hope they come to get us out," Taylor said when he and Grace were back in the warm car.

"Of course they will," Grace said. "What an idea."

"They're mad I didn't help," Taylor said. "And now this. They'll blame me. You'll see."

"That's all in your mind," Grace said. "Look," she said, "I'm sorry about sitting in that kid's lap. I thought I was playing the old married woman to the hilt. I thought it would amuse you. I thought you'd be as pleased with me as I was."

"I see," Taylor said. "I didn't see then, but I see now. It's really all right. I just wish I could go back over it again and laugh in the right place." He didn't feel at all like laughing as he began to understand the vast sadness of the gap between his game of the Mann Act and her game of the old married couple, but he did feel a new and very different tenderness toward her. He wondered how much of all that she knew. "I really feel as if we have been married for a long long time," he said. Then, carried away, he added what he thought for a moment might not be a lie, "I think really I was upset at the thought we hadn't been."

"Oh, Ross—"she said. She put her hand on his sleeve, but he didn't trust himself to touch her, not there, not then, not any longer.

"It's just too bad," she said.

"Please, don't touch me," he said. His hands clutched the wheel as they had all day.

She withdrew her hand but was still near him on the seat. Then he heard the boys coming up the trail. He hurriedly put his arm around her shoulders and gave her a gentle squeeze. It really was like squeezing a woman he had been married to for a long long time: they had been through a lot together and small signs meant much. When the boys began to appear out of the gloom, he put his hands back on the wheel.

"We'll laugh about this sometime," she said.

Taylor was glad it was dark because he wasn't laughing then. He could feel his eyes brimming, and he was afraid the tears would start to shine down his cheeks at any minute. They didn't—not then and not on the long ride up through a corner of Vermont and down to the Albany station and not even at the station where she caught last night's train coming through six hours late—and that at least was something.

He thought about that day on every New Year's for the rest of his life and at strange moments in between, but he never once laughed about it.

Who, What, When, Where— Why?

Now this is a story I've tried to tell a good many times, but I've always managed to get something wrong. It never comes out the way I want it to, but what's worse, it never comes out at all. I don't know that any story has ever come out exactly the way I wanted it to, but they usually manage to come out some way or other, sometimes a little better, sometimes a little worse than I wanted. Sometimes they surprise me and come out in a way I never imagined, much much better than what I had in mind to begin with. I pretend, of course, that I planned it all and take whatever credit the story has coming to it. It's only fair. I need a lot of credit I haven't earned to balance my losses on stories like this, stories that never come out with all my planning, all my imagination, insight, even fragments of those mysterious outcroppings of forgotten dreams we call—sometimes— inspiration.

I've moved the story around a good deal in the various drafts. I've had it happen in Tuscaloosa, Alabama, which is a real place, and Randalla, Alabama, which isn't. I've had it happen in Korea and Vietnam. I've had it happen in Africa—moved back, of course, in time so that it looked like a Conrad story—because one of the basic requirements of the story is that it be in a place where there are people who can be identified as Natives or Gooks or A-rabs—there was one version set in some city of the Middle East, but I had to look that up and have forgotten where it was. I wish Conrad had written the story and got it out of my way or that I could read *Heart of Dark-*

ness as coming close enough to what this story has been trying to say.

The one thing I haven't tried with the story is telling it exactly the way it happened. So, first, this happened in Birmingham, Alabama, which is both a real and an imaginary place. That is, you can look it up on a map and find out about it in an encyclopedia. You can write letters to it and make long distance calls. You can visit your travel agent, and he will sell you tickets and book you into the Howard Johnson Motel unless you remember to specify the Tutwiler Hotel, where the action is—or was anyway—on football weekends. They used to move all the furniture out of the lobby to get ready for the stampede and to make sure we couldn't sleep on the sofas. All that is very real but it also helps explain Birmingham as an imaginary place: I don't think I was ever sober in Birmingham.

We used to go up for the football weekends, naturally, but we also managed to get up for a weekend now and then during the rest of the year. We'd go up on Friday afternoon and come back on Sunday. I can remember sleeping in cars parked behind a hotel, and I can remember sleeping on the floor behind a velvet (and very dusty) curtain in a hotel ballroom. But sleep wasn't a very big item on those weekends. I don't really remember what we did, but whatever it was, it kept us from sleeping.

There was a hotel where we drank. I'd like to say it was the Allerton but that name may have drifted in from other and much later associations. A hotel bar, anyway. A hotel by no means first class. There was a sign on the wall over our favorite booth: Corkage Fee—but I don't remember what the fee was. Probably a quarter. I haven't seen one of those signs for so long that perhaps I'd better explain that although it was absolutely illegal to bring a bottle of whiskey into a bar—only beer was sold—the management would charge you a quarter if you did it. There was another sign that made it clearer: Out of Respect for State and Local Police Officers, Please Keep Your Bottle off the Table. What you did was keep it in a paper bag on the bench side of you. Oh, the folkways, the little maneuvers you don't get a chance to show off any more, the skills, like pissing on a train without making a mess of yourself.

Perhaps one reason we drank in that particular bar was that upstairs, on the seventh floor, there was a whorehouse. We couldn't always afford the whores, but it was nice to think they were there. I remember now that I once got a good night's sleep in a whore's bed. For some reason she never came into the room, and I was left undisturbed. I expect she got a better offer. It wouldn't have had to be very good, she knew.

The mention of Conrad and Korea and Vietnam shows, I guess, that the time has moved around as much as the place. In addition to 1890, 1952, 1966, there is a kind of all-purpose timeless present in which the protagonist, after living among Gooks for many years, comes home to the Land of the Free only to discover that the Native problem there is as bad as anywhere—worse, because now it is his problem.

This protagonist, for some reason, is often an engineer. No, that "for some reason" is evasive. Probably downright dishonest. At the very least lazy. There is an engineer in me somewhere, a very young man preserved in amber exactly as he was when I flunked out of M.I.T. And that is exactly the age at which this really happened, so the engineer, unlikely as it seems, is perhaps the one honest thing in all those versions. He is never such a very young man, of course. He ages right along with me, I notice, but being an engineer he is just one step closer to that very young man who got left behind in the shuffle of things working themselves out. I have always been kind to him and made him a very successful engineer and a deeply concerned man. What else could I do? When he is in the army, he is an army engineer, but then there is too much else going on to keep the issues clear, so those versions abort pretty quickly. An engineer is what he has always been until now when I am sending him all the way back to be an undergraduate on a weekend spree in Birmingham, Alabama, on a winter night in 1938.

I don't remember exactly when it was. It wasn't a football weekend. It wasn't warm. In other versions I would just pick a day, February 13, 1939, for example, checking only to make sure that February 13 fell on a weekend in 1939. And so much for verisimilitude. The theory is OK, so it must be something else that kept the story from working. Getting the date right surely wasn't enough to save it.

Nor were the fine authentic names taken from the telephone book or from the spines of books in my bookcase: Conrad Henry, Joseph James, James Madox, Henry Ford, the possibilities are endless.

The cast of characters is made up, in addition to I, of two undergraduates, one steel mill worker, one Negro, male—I'm trying to get back to what really happened, so I must call him a Negro, although I know that he ought to be called a Black—one Negro, male, with blood dripping from his chin onto his white shirt, one Negro, female, wringing her hands. As clearly as in the newest style of subtitles I see the words "She is wringing her hands." I think I heard them at the time. She is the only person I have ever seen actually wring her hands—outside of the movies, of course. And a small group of Negroes, male. A half-dozen of them, I believe, but quite undifferentiated. I think one of the mistakes I made in some of the other versions was to try to make them individuals, which resulted in an assortment of quick stereotypes. I apologize to Blacks, although the error was artistic rather than social. That is all. There were no onlookers, no policemen, no U.S. Cavalry, no deus—nor diabolus—ex machina.

It is the business of I to make himself known, so nothing further will be said about him. Among the remaining characters, far and away the most important is the one labeled until now First College Boy. His name is Gordy Stuart. He is one of the worst men I have ever known. I have in my head a constantly changing list of candidates for Mr. Awful, and his name has never dropped off the list. Army sergeants, department heads, deans, conniving colleagues, public figures come and go on the list but Gordy Stuart is always there. He was my roommate my freshman year at Alabama, and he was perhaps the first really awful person I had ever had to know.

What strikes me as curious at this minute is why I have never tried to write anything about him. He has never appeared in any of these stories. Even in this version he has only one awful line to speak, and now that I think the versions over I find that that one line has invariably gravitated toward the protagonist, I. It is said ironically, hysterically, never straight, but it is always said and it is said by the protagonist.

As soon as I start thinking about Gordy Stuart, I start inventing explanations for his character. If I were to write about him, I think I might make him like Stephen Crane's Swede in "The Blue Hotel," who behaves so outrageously only because he is frightened to death. I think I might show Gordy overcompensating for an inferiority complex. You have to do that sort of thing in a story, but what I am trying to get at here is what really happened, and for that there is no explanation possible. Not that it matters, because no explanation can ever change what Gordy Stuart has meant to me all these years and probably always will mean.

It was just a fluke that he walked into the room I had rented. We introduced ourselves, and then he put his bag down on the other bed. I don't know what he was thinking, but I was almost overcome with joy to find that here, a thousand miles from home, I had lucked into a roommate from Massachusetts. To be sure, he lived about thirty miles north of Boston and I lived about thirty miles south, but at a distance of a thousand miles, that was nothing. Naturally I had heard of Haverhill, because that's a big enough city to be heard of, and, besides, I'm pretty sure that the hero of some series of boys' books lived there. I would have known for sure when I was a freshman. Equally naturally he had never heard of East Bridgewater. Anybody who says he has has got to be lying or at least have it mixed up with Bridgewater, where there is a teachers' college and a rather notorious prison.

Gordy was awful from the beginning, but I didn't know that's what it was. I was only intimidated. I saw that he was handsome, and I saw that he considered himself handsome. The best I hoped for myself was that some day Beauty would kiss me and I would become handsome, but I didn't allow myself to think much about it. So Gordy depressed the hell out of me. He had what I remember as the best complexion I have ever seen, a clear pink and white that would be the despair of women in periods when natural complexion was in vogue. He was well built, about six-two, I'd say. I don't really know, although he was always giving us his statistics. One hundred and ninety pounds, perhaps. He had a slight stammer and moved in a strange brusque way as if he were throwing his arms and legs at you.

He said he had been an all-state tackle on last year's team, and it was maybe twenty-five years before I thought to doubt his word.

Since domestic murders are usually touched off, I am told, by events quite trivial in themselves, I will simply say that the thing I still hate him for is the way he would run home between classes and read my Boston *Post*, which came in the mail every day. The next year when we were no longer roommates he still went by my house and tore the wrapper off my *Post* until I canceled the subscription out of spite. I remember that vividly but I don't remember why I said to him one night while we were roommates, "All right, if that's what you want, we'll go outside and settle it, but I'm taking this poker with me because one of us isn't coming back." I can't believe I meant it, but he didn't care to check it out. I don't remember that it made any difference in our relationship.

Of course, the thing that most depressed me was his success with girls. He would hold court in our room in the evening describing how he fucked this one and banged that one and screwed the one and plowed the other and, what was more, pissed on the one who was such a pig. The only time we double-dated—he had arranged it all—they were both pigs to my way of thinking, and my date and I sat on the edge of the Lock throwing stones into the river while Gordy and his date used the Drive-It. That one he "screwed till she begged for mercy." That was his style. My date and I mutually declined the pleasure, and Gordy and I took them back to the dorm after the shortest possible ritual coke. Well, that's Gordon Stuart, First College Student.

Second College Student was a friend of Gordy's, Billy McHugh. They had gone to the same high school, although Billy was a couple of years older. Their friendship seemed based more on a local pool hall than on the high school. Billy was quite small, five-four or -five I would say. His face was soft and round and should have been jolly but was, in fact, severe and thoughtful like a midget's. He said he had a very bad heart, and he rested a lot to save whatever evergy he had for drinking and screwing. He rarely went to class. I liked him much better than Gordy, probably because he was quieter. However, he didn't have the good sense you might expect of a person so quiet and watchful. About the middle of our first year, he was thrown out of the house for not showing enough respect to the landlord. I must admit that I thought it strange that an old man like that should go with us to Birmingham and drink and screw right along with us. He was, in fact, in his mid-seventies, so it never occurred to me to call him anything but sir even when I was packing him on my back through the middle of Birmingham on a Sunday morning, dead drunk, screwed into a coma, through the crowds of people on their way to church. Billy, on the other hand, thought that fucking the same whore established certain rights. He couldn't have been more wróng. He called that venerable whoremaster George just once and was packed and out of the house by sundown.

I don't know where the old man was on this occasion. If we didn't use his car, we rarely got to Birmingham. Perhaps he was upstairs. Very likely. After all, he was the only one of us who could afford to indulge himself to his heart's content. If he and I had been alone, he would perhaps have stood treat for me, but he never did it for the lot of us, although he could have afforded that, too. I think even then he didn't much like the other two. He might very well have seen that George looming on the horizon.

So there are the First and Second College Students and the Narrator. I guess the Steel Worker comes next. This is the first time he has ever been a steel worker, probably because the story has never been laid in Birmingham before. I've known him to be a truck driver, an off-duty cop, a construction worker, a Green Beret. But he was, in fact, a steel worker from the tin mill in Bessemer, still in his hard hat and very dirty. The characters are beginning to flatten out about here. I don't even remember where we picked him up. If I were just doing another version of the story instead of trying to re-cord what actually happened, I would have the three of us sitting at the table under the sign Corkage Fee 25 Cents. Behind the bar next to the cash register there would be a big calendar: March 18, 1938. We would have our bottle tucked into the corner of the booth—in a brown paper bag, of course. At this point in the story, we would have come down from upstairs and have had time for a drink or perhaps two.

Gordy: M-miss.

Waitress: (Calls from behind counter.) Yes, sir?

Gordy: Set-ups, please.

Waitress: Anything else?

Billy: A barbeque for me.

Waitress: Anything else?

Gordy: G-goddamn, why not? How about the small steak?

Waitress: How do you want it?

Gordy: Like I want all my pieces of ass, rare.

Waitress: Anything else?

I: No, thank you.

Now at this time, Enter, Man in Work Clothes. Actually he has been sitting at the counter, half turned so he can observe the three in the booth. His name is always a Southern-type name, Billy Joe or B. J., for example. The trouble is that I've never been able to score the name properly. It will keep coming out B period J period Johns full stop when it should come out in the rhythm of demijohn. I think I should confess that the names are given with a certain malice. Before that year I had never heard names like Billy Joe or B. J. or Betty Sue, and I thought them distinctly odd, even contemptible, I'm afraid. Having myself just progressed from Danny to Dan, I scorned men who had never made it all the way to a man's name. Women, too. So I suspect that when some character shows up with a name like Willy when he should be Will or with some double-barreled diminutive, I'm having at him. Anyway, B. J. Johns prepares to take part in the conversation.

Billy: This will about finish the whiskey.

Gordy: S-state store's closed by now, too.

I: What will we do? (Privately glad not to have to spend more money and try to keep down more whiskey.)

B. J.: (Approaches table.) Gentlemen.

Gordy: Sir?

B. J.: I believe I can help you.

Billy: You got some whiskey?

B. J.: No, but I know where I can get some.

Billy: Sit down, sit down.

Gordy: M-miss, another set-up.

Waitress: (Putting four set-ups on table.) I'm way ahead of you.

As I say, however, I don't know how it was that the Steel Worker got mixed up with us. But there is no doubt he was sitting in the booth with us, helping us finish our whiskey. After a while we were all out in the street, but it would be nonsense to assume, as I have in all versions up to this one, that we were going to get whiskey. Even I knew that if we wanted whiskey all we had to do was speak to the same elevator man we spoke to when we wanted women. So it must have been while we were still sitting in the booth that Gordy said the one thing I am sure anyone said that night. We must have just finished the whiskey.

Gordy: Let's go kill us a nigger.

The Steel Worker stood up without a word and led us into the street. The street was as deserted as a dream, and I had the dream feeling that everybody who wasn't there knew something I didn't know. It's the feeling you have on the Interstate when you haven't seen a car for five minutes that feel like a week. I had it on the main street of Jackson, Mississippi, about midnight just a few days back.

We turned a corner onto another deserted street and began staggering, arm in arm, into the solitude. Then, not very far away, a man and a woman, arm in arm, turned a corner and came toward us. Not entirely satisfied with my dealings with the whore, I envied them. They were Black. The Steel Worker broke from Gordy's arm and knocked the man down.

Tableau: Steel Worker in hard hat, standing, legs wide, fists ready. Black Man, excessively bright blood on his white shirt, standing in the doorway of a store, reflected back and forth in show windows. Black Woman, wringing her hands. Three College Students, aghast.

In all fairness to Gordy, I must say that he had no idea that what he said meant anything. He used the expression all the time. On the other hand, he was one of those Northerners who found/find an emotional home in the South. Part of his awfulness was his racial bigotry, and he didn't have the personal experience or the social tradition to allow him to disguise it as anything else. In dealing with Blacks, he was worse than any Southerner I ever knew. I might be able to invent an explanation, but I don't know one.

Now things begin to jump around. There is a gap. The Blacks have disappeared. The four of us are alone. We are at a corner and can see for blocks in all directions. Absolutely nothing is moving. There is not even a banner flapping to suggest the nostalgia of the infinite: we are right there and nowhere else, and there is nothing but us.

We walk very quietly down the block. We still stagger a little but it is all pretense.

Suddenly I am looking at the other three running. They run very fast. They run in different directions. Several streets meet there, and in Europe someone would have put up a statue or even a fountain. But in this scene it is just more and bigger emptiness with three men running off into three different streets. I am looking at their backs, but I know that their mouths are open in the attitude of screaming. Very silent, of course.

I am looking at all this, I realize, over a man's shoulder. I realize it is a shoulder in a white shirt spotted with excessively red blood. I realize also that blood is dripping off the handle of a knife onto my hand. I realize that the blade of the knife is grating against my teeth through my upper lip. I decide to lie down. But I am held up by a fierce and sullen group of men. They are Black, of course.

At this point, various things have been known to happen. I have, by a ruse, escaped and run off after the others. Usually, however, I am beaten very badly and left for the police to find. I have usually given myself the virtue of refusing to testify against anybody and have given myself in addition some such line as "No, they weren't Natives."

The truth is that I don't know how those men and I ever came unstuck. How that knife ever got out of my lip. Which is very unfortunate when it comes to story values, because you can scarcely hope to write a story in which a group like that is forever stuck together and a knife like that is forever grating on your teeth.

The Great Day

It was St. Patrick's Day of Mike Pegnam's first year in New York. Three hundred and sixty-four days out of the year he could take Irishness or leave it alone, but on that day he liked to stand up and be counted. On that day he was willing frankly to close up his shop and put a card on his door saying that he was sorry and would be back tomorrow. On that day people could look at his card and say, So that's the kind of name Pegnam is. I always thought it was French.

Unfortunately he didn't have a shop of his own to close up, so that year he had to concentrate on defrauding the company just a little more than usual. He had prepared very carefully for St. Patrick's Day over a long time. He had called on every architect, engineer, contractor, banker, real estate operator in his territory just to make sure that there was nothing that would break on March 17 and show that he wasn't on the job. As a result the company got almost a month of hard work out of him, and good will in his territory was the best it had been in over a year. The net result of his work, however, was that he discovered what he already knew: things were dead.

But on the morning of March 17 his conscience was good. Outside of a couple of items he noticed in the newspaper on the way to work, there was only one thing he had to check before the decks would be completely clear for the day and very likely for some days to come. He got to the office early and by nine o'clock he was on the telephone talking to Miss Rossi of Palazzo and Murphy, general contractors.

She had promised him a report on the opening of bids for a convent and school in Rome-on-Hudson, New York. As a matter of fact she did much better than that. Not only did Palazzo and Murphy get the Rome job, but they were bidding as well on a monastery at Ithaca (the Buffalo office should have picked that up first) and on a convent-mission at Tuscaloosa, Alabama, a job which after lying dormant for years had evidently come to life just when the Atlanta office had forgotten all about it. That made three good reports, especially since two of them made the other offices look bad. Miss Rossi also gave him no-progress reports on two cathedrals, a burned rectory, a gymnasium, a church, an orphanage, a retreat house, and a pizzeria—this last job she passed on her way to work, and she was keeping her eye on it for him.

Actually, on the basis of his talk with Miss Rossi, he could have knocked off for the day. Things were so tough that there were many days when a reporter got far less than he had already got, but he wanted to make it look unusually good before he headed for McSorley's and St. Patrick's Day. He made a couple more calls and got a project-completed on an apartment house and an electrical subcontractor on a restaurant renovation.

He had finished typing up all the reports and was just pulling himself together to go out into his territory when Jimmy Schyler, his immediate boss, came over with a newspaper. "Here's a present for you," Jimmy said. Mike took the paper and stared glumly at the circled item. "Don't get sore," Jimmy said. Jimmy wasn't a bad guy for a boss even if he did sniff whenever he came near Mike's desk after lunch and laugh self-consciously and shake his head and say McSalty's.

"OK," Mike said. "What creep dug this up?" The paper was a local Long Island paper, and the item recorded the transfer of property in Great Neck to one Amandio Giavi, whose address unfortunately was just inside the lower boundary of Mike's territory and way over by the North River.

"Don't get sore at me," Jimmy said. "I know it stinks. But one of the big boys on the twenty-second floor came up with me on the elevator and gave it to me. 'See what your boys can do with this,' he says. 'I'll be watching the service,' he says. So we got to get out some kind of report. See what you can do anyway."

Mike said, "OK," and sat down with his hat and coat on. Jimmy stood beside him for a minute playing with his fingers and then, evidently remembering something important, rushed back into his office. Mike picked up his tattered Manhattan directory and found to his relief that Amandio Giavi had a telephone.

Mike let the phone ring half a dozen times, each ring increasing his assurance that he had done his best. Relieved, he pinned the clipping to a report form, added the telephone number, and scrawled CHECK SITE across the whole form. He stood up, dropped the thing into the out basket for the Long Island reporter, and ostentatiously took up his briefcase.

Jimmy was peering out of his cubbyhole as Mike went by. "Going out?" he said.

"Uh," Mike said. He kept going.

"Get anything on Giavi?"

"Nuh." He wasn't fast enough. Jimmy bounded out with a sheaf of papers in his hand and walked along to the elevators.

"Well, drop everything else and get down there. See Giavi if you can. Try to find somebody who knows what he's going to do. The heat's really on both of us."

"OK," Mike said. "If that's the way you want it, Jimmy."

Jimmy reached up and patted Mike's shoulder. "Good stuff," he said.

"I'll have to go back for a minute," Mike said.

"OK," Jimmy said. "On the ball." He went on to the elevators.

Mike went back and picked the clipping and all the other reports out of the basket and stuffed them into his briefcase. Of course this Giavi deal would have to come up just when he had everything so well organized. It would take time to get to that address, and at an address like that it would take time, very likely, to find Giavi, and then with a name like that it might take time to explain to him what was wanted. Mike's lunch at McSorley's would suffer and his St. Patrick's Day would suffer. He would suffer. And by God if he had to suffer the company would suffer too. That's what he had in mind when he took all the reports out of the basket. If he had to spend the whole day on Giavi, the company couldn't expect him to get anything else; therefore he could hold off on the Rossi material for a day and go to the show the next day. Those reports would cover him one day as well as another.

He must have been scowling worse than usual because when Jimmy met him at the elevators he said, "Just do your best. Don't worry."

"Don't worry," Mike said. The door closed between them and Mike went down to the street.

Mike was so mad that he even forgot to check the restaurant remodeling in the ground floor of the company's own building. The big bosses saw it every day as they came in, and they checked the service first thing every morning to make sure that the reporter (Mike) was getting the subcontracts as they were awarded.

He crossed over to a Nedick's and savagely downed a double orange juice and then recklessly another. Even as he was doing it he realized that it wasn't a very effective gesture, but it was the best at hand. Then he plunged underground and stashed his hat, coat, and briefcase in a locker. He boarded that wonderful BMT, the subway that runs diagonally where everything else is at right angles, and was shortly at Eighth Street on the East Side.

As he walked into McSorley's two ideas hit him almost at once. First he thought, Home at last. And then he thought, I forgot Giavi. For the slow moment that he stood just inside the door while his eyes became accustomed to the dimness, he remembered that he had forgotten to check Giavi's address. He had a nagging feeling that he wouldn't be able to forget Giavi again as he had angrily forgotten him while he was the very cause of his anger.

Even as he stepped toward the bar, Mike saw that McSorley's around him wasn't the place he had hoped it would be. It wasn't the place that it was all the other days of the year. It wasn't the place that by being just what it was could be so much more in conjunction with a day like St. Patrick's Day. It was more crowded than it had any right to be, and most of the people he didn't know although by then he was a regular. He stepped up to the bar, however, walking gingerly on the green sawdust, which was the first thing that had come into his sight after his eyes had changed.

As he was waiting for the bartender to get to him, he saw that the walls were festooned with green crepe paper and that the tables, the good stained scarred tables, were covered with paper tablecloths, white with green harps and shamrocks. He noticed with some pleasure that the tablecloths were already beginning to disintegrate where wet mugs had been set on them. The bartender wasn't getting to him, and he was thinking that maybe it would be better later and that maybe Giavi could be fitted in about then. Then Harry, the proprietor, came through the crowd and stood beside him for a moment, putting a hand on his shoulder. "Good morning, Mike," Harry said.

"Good morning, Harry," Mike said.

"Where's your mug?" Harry said.

"I haven't been able to get one yet," Mike said.

"Otto," Harry shouted, "one for Mike." His red face streaming with sweat, Otto trotted the length of the bar with an ale and without saying a word trotted back to the tap, his white shirt dark across his back. Mike took a good swig of ale. It at least was what it always was. "A great day, Mike," Harry said, and patting Mike's shoulder again, he walked off through the crowd.

"A great day, Harry," Mike called after him. Harry only waved his hand without looking back. Mike drank off the rest of his ale, for he was very thirsty. He had no trouble getting the next ale, for Otto was by then working that end of the bar. He left his money on the bar and Otto kept dipping into it.

When it got along toward twelve o'clock, Mike carried his mug over to the small table near the telephone booth, one of McSorley's few concessions to the twentieth century. His dripping mug made the green of the tablecloth run, and he got it on his hands. He wiped his hands on a plain paper napkin, all the while looking comfortably and leisurely across the room at the big picture of the the nude, which hangs there for men to look at whenever they please without being afraid that some woman will catch them looking at a picture of a naked woman.

The telephone rang, and Mario the waiter, who happened to be passing, leaned into the booth and answered it. He looked across the room. "Gonzales," he shouted. "Gonzales." No one answered and Mario hung up the receiver without speaking into the phone again.

That reminded Mike of Giavi, and he gave the number another try, but no one answered. When he came out of the booth, a great plate of corned beef and cabbage and half a loaf of bread were ready on the table. But the meal was spoiled for him because he couldn't forget Giavi. Whether he looked at the woman in the picture or at his plate he couldn't forget him. He couldn't forget him even when he watched the older men at their ease at the table under the picture. That table was tacitly the head table, and Mike had been hoping for some time now to be invited to sit at it, but evidently he hadn't been around long enough although Harry addressed him by name and the cook allowed him to go out into the kitchen to order for himself, a privilege of the regulars.

When he had finished his lunch, Mike decided that the only way to forget Giavi was to get over to the address and finish it off one way or another. He was on his way out when he met Harry. "Not staying for the singing?" Harry said.

"I've got a little business," Mike said, "but I'll be right back. I've never been in New York before for the Day."

Harry nodded wisely. "It's a great day," he said.

"A great day," Mike said.

"Try to get back," Harry said. "Jimmy said he'd be sure to drop in for a couple of songs, and there'll be others too. Billy O'Neil, for instance."

"A fine voice for Irish songs," Mike said.

"When he doesn't pitch it too high," Harry said. Mike knew that as well as Harry did, but he knew it wasn't for him to say, so he just nodded and went on out.

Although Mike had had only six ales with his lunch, two more than his ordinary working-day allowance, he felt most pleasantly irresponsible now that he had made up his mind. The sunlight was something of a shock, but he carried enough of McSorley's dim quiet with him so that it didn't bother him too much. He even felt a little condescending toward the company as he walked across town to have a look at this Giavi.

It started out to be a pleasant walk, but after a while he had no more idea where he was going than a dog and no more awareness of what was around him than a tree. He woke up in the meat-packing section of Fourteenth Street, and he knew he must be getting close to the address he wanted.

The door, when he finally found it after three passes up and down the block, was gray in a gray wall. The metal numbers had been painted over and were gray like the rest. There were no windows in the building on the street level, and those on the floors above were too dirty to see through. He opened the door fearfully.

A broad flight of stairs went up into the gloom. The stairs started right at the door, and by the time he was well inside he was several steps up so that he had some difficulty reaching down to pull the door shut after him. With the door shut he was in such complete darkness that he crept back down and opened the door again to get the lay of the land before going on up. Once out on the sidewalk he took a good look at the stairs. On each of the risers as far up as he could see a sign was painted, evidently indicating the tenants of the building. None of the signs he could see had to do with Giavi or his business. He saw signs for tailors and lawyers. There was even a sign for a general contracting firm he visited in Rockefeller Plaza. He got down on his hands and knees on the sidewalk and tried to read the sign on the first riser, but it had been so kicked and scuffed by people stumbling over the bottom step that it was illegible.

He went in and pulled the door in after him and went on up the stairs resolutely. He had already spent too much time on the Giavi deal. When at last he stumbled off the top of the stairs and stood looking around, he saw, both to left and right, a patch of dim light coming from a dirty window. There was a distant hum of machinery and he could feel the floor tremble under his feet. He went to the left for no reason but that he thought the sound of the machinery came from that direction. He walked all the way to the window without finding a door that felt as if it had been opened in thirty years. When he reached the window he saw that instead of being at the end of the corridor he was really at a bend and that in the distance another dim patch of light came through another dirty window.

Not wanting to get lost in the darkness, he reversed his steps and walked back toward the window at the right of the stairs. He found nothing in that direction either except another bend in the corridor. There it seemed to him that the sound of the machines was louder, but he could see no light coming through in the distance. As he stood hesitating, the sound of the machines swelled and sank quickly as if someone had opened and closed a door. One more try, he told himself, would rid him of Giavi.

He was very soon beyond the small light of the dirty window and in complete darkness. With his fingertips he followed the wall. Twice he sprang back as his fingers punched into nothing. Each time he told himself it was an open door. Once some great bug ran over his hand, and he stood still for a moment with his heart in suspension. He would have quit then, but he had to convince himself that he wouldn't quit for a bug.

He forced himself to step forward and very nearly broke his neck on a short flight of steps. As he tried to get up he put his hand on something that felt horribly like a man's face. He didn't dare move his hand, but whatever it was didn't move as he rested on it. Mike shifted his weight and stealthily moved his hand away and groped for a match. The light of the match showed only too clearly that it was a man he had touched. His mouth tasted as if he were eating a handful of pennies. He leaned down for a good look.

The man sat up suddenly, stared around quickly, blew a great stinking winy breath in Mike's face, and fell back again, hitting his head a tremendous thump on the floor. He began to snore loudly.

Mike picked himself up and got the hell out of there.

The next thing he knew he was sitting in a phone booth drinking beer with a little whiskey on the side. The receiver was hanging on its cord, and from time to time he would pick it up and listen to the ringing of the phone on the other end.

And then he had been walking a long time, and he felt a little sick with the last fire of the burned-out whiskey flickering hotly in his gut. And then he was in front of McSorley's.

As Mike first went into McSorley's he saw that the man with the fiddle was there. He wasn't playing at the moment but arguing loudly about Mother Machree. His one good eye fixed his opponent, and his fierce glass eye stared off at an angle, holding the rest of the room at bay. He was sitting in front of the telephone booth, so Mike had to squeeze around behind him to get in. As Mike was dialing Giavi's number he could see that the kitchen was closed and that the head table was filled with people he had never seen before. The telephone rang half a dozen times. Then at the other end of the line the receiver was snatched up and someone shouted, "Giavi talking." Mike could hear machines in the background.

"Webster Building Reports," Mike said.

"What's that?" the man shouted. "This is Giavi talking."

"I'm calling for Webster Building Reports," Mike said a little louder and much more clearly.

"Turn the goddamn things off." This shout nearly tore his ear off. Mike held the receiver at arm's length, but when he listened again he could hear the machines running down as if they had been shut off. "Webster?" Giavi said—it was really a reduced shout. "What do you want, Webster? Want to sell me a dictionary?"

"No, Mr. Giavi. This is another Webster." People were always thinking he sold dictionaries.

"Well, what have you got, Webster? Cigars? Talk up."

"No," Mike said, "not that Webster either." Although not so many people would think of that most people he came in contact with seemed to know it well enough to make a joke.

The man with the fiddle had his head in the telephone booth. "Quiet, quiet," he screamed. "We can't hear ourselves sing."

"Sorry," Mike whispered.

"What's that?" Giavi shouted. "What's that? Talk to me, Webster. What's your proposition?"

"Mr. Giavi," Mike said, "we publish a daily bulletin of interest to the building trades. Our subscribers want to know about building that is planned or is actually being done."

"OK. OK. So what?"

"I see by the paper," Mike said, "that you have bought property in Great Neck."

"So what?" His shout was becoming louder and more distracting. "OK. So what?"

"So if you could give us some information concerning your plans for the property—" Mike was beginning to sweat in the telephone booth.

"Why? Why? Why?"

"Our subscribers," Mike said, "who are contractors and material suppliers, will contact you and make competitive bids so that you can get the work done most cheaply and efficiently."

"No," Giavi shouted, "no, I don't know you. I don't want to buy any."

"But, Mr. Giavi, I'm not selling anything."

"Quiet," shrieked the head of the man with the fiddle. One eye stared fiercely at Mike. The other glared down the throat of the telephone as if to put Giavi out of countenance. Mike edged around with his back to him. He slammed the door on Mike's back.

"Mr. Giavi—"

"Non capisco inglese."

"Please, Mr. Giavi, listen to me."

"I don't want any."

"Mr. Giavi—"

"Start them up," Giavi shouted. The telephone trembled in Mike's hand. The machines cut in again in full cry.

"Mr. Giavi." Mike raised his voice. "Mr. Giavi, let me tell you again." He could hear only the machines. The door of the telephone booth beat against his back. "Can you hear me, Mr. Giavi?" Mike heard his voice softly under the sound of the machines. "I can't hear you, Mr. Giavi," he shouted. There was a click, then only the hum of a dead phone.

As Mike started out of the booth, the man with the fiddle blocked his way. "What's the idea?" the man said. "Huh?"

"What's the idea with you?" Mike said. "Yelling at me when I'm trying to do business over the telephone so loud I can't hear what he says."

"What's the idea yelling so loud we can't hear ourselves sing?" the man said, one eye fixing Mike and the other looking to the rest of the room for support.

"I have to do my business," Mike said.

"Business, business," the man shouted. And they glared at each other. Mike's heart wasn't really in it, but he didn't want the man to get away with anything. The man's face was getting redder by the minute. "Business," he shouted again and glared so hard that the eye that was looking at Mike jumped right out of its socket and rolled on the floor in the green sawdust.

They both got down on their hands and knees to look for it. There were ten or twelve of them on their hands and knees when Harry came over with a huge handful of mugs. "Drink up, boys," he said. "No hard feelings on Paddy's Day." He gave them each a mug and they sat on the floor drinking their ale and running the green sawdust through their fingers looking for the glass eye. The man with the fiddle finally found it in a big drift of sawdust in the corner, and they all stood up and sang "Danny Boy."

Mike moved over to the bar for a while because he had a long way to go before he would feel good again. As he was settling down at the bar, an old man near the door began calling querulously for Harry. Several other old men stood up and seeing what was happening took up the call: Woman, Harry, Woman. And Harry ran to tell the woman, No women, and the old men settled down again.

Mike was feeling pretty low what with Giavi and the man with the fiddle and the alcohol that was going away and leaving him flat. He tossed off a couple of quick ales, but it didn't seem to help much. About that time the man with the saxophone came out of the back room. Mike hadn't seen him go in, but there he was coming out with his saxophone under his arm and his saucer in his hand. Mike put a dime in the saucer and turned a fish eye on the man next to him, and whether it was because of that or not, the man put a quarter in the saucer. The man with the saxophone tilted change, saucer, and all into the pocket of his jacket. He tipped his hat to the room at large and went out into the street. Mike watched the face of the man next to him.

"But he didn't play a note," the man said.

"No," Mike said, "he never does."

In much better spirits he began tossing off ale after ale. He caught up on the sickness he had been feeling and left it far behind in a new cycle of exhilaration. He thought briefly of checking in at the office, but he knew that the office had been closed for hours. It must have been about then that the fiddle started "Kevin Barry" and he went over and made up a quartet with three clean-looking fellows he had been watching for some time as they sang song after song aggressively. He put his head in between two of the singers' heads, and they put their arms around his shoulders: another martyr for old Ireland, another murder for the crown.

They had sung for a long time and had drunk a number of ales with the fiddle player, who seemed not to remember any previous trouble. "Let's get the hell out of here," one of the singers said. "Too damn many foreigners. They don't have any business coming into McSorley's on a day like this."

"OK by me," Mike said. These seemed like good guys and he wanted to find out more about them, especially as they had an accent he couldn't quite place.

"Let's go then," one of them said.

"Will you wait while I make a phone call?" Mike said.

"Hurry," one of them said.

"We'll wait," another said.

Mike went into the booth and dialed a number. He was pretty drunk by then, and he didn't know what number he dialed or who he was supposed to be calling, but as he sat listening to the phone ring and ring and ring, he realized that he was calling Giavi. He could see himself dialing the number as clearly as if he were still doing it, so he hung up. Then for no reason he called information to find out if there was a phone listed for Giavi in Great Neck. And there was. At the address he had.

The phone was answered on the first ring. A very solemn-sounding man said, "Mr. Giavi's residence."

"J. T. Webster Corporation," Mike said. That's how the manual said to get past characters like him. It was supposed to sound just a little too impressive to brush off.

"Just a minute," the man said.

"Giavi talking."

"Webster Building Reports," Mike said.

"Can you hear me now, Webster?" Mike recognized the voice although Giavi was now speaking very quietly.

"Fine, Mr. Giavi. I can hear you fine." He must have shouted it because he saw the man with the fiddle glare at him over his shoulder.

"OK, Webster?"

"Yes, Mr. Giavi, I hear you fine."

"Drop dead," he said and hung up.

Mike put up the phone and opened the door of the booth. Two of his boys grabbed him by the arms, and they were out in the street before he could so much as say, I think I'd rather not. By the time they had got over to Third Avenue, he had at least found out who his friends were. Two were in the British Merchant Marine. One of those was Cuddles, from Liverpool. The other was Danny, from Cobh. That was a real discovery to discover a real Irishman on St. Patrick's Day. The third guy was named Bud, and he only talked like that because he happened to be with a couple of foreigners. At that Mike couldn't blame him because he found himself putting on a thick brogue.

Cuddles and Danny went running up and down the street yelling for the driver of a parked cab. Mike and this guy Bud leaned up against the Cooper Union and watched the other two casting back and forth like hounds on a scent. All of a sudden Bud said, "I'm on to you, so blow."

"What's this?" Mike said, coming back from a long way off.

"I'm on to your game. But I got there first, so blow."

"Speak up or shut up," Mike said. He thought it might be a good idea to sound tough.

"I found these two," Bud said. "I been working on them half the day, and when they pass out I'm going to be the one who rolls them, not some guy who just happens along like you, so blow."

"We'll see about that," Mike said. He twitched his shoulders inside his coat to give Bud something to think about. He knew he looked pretty big in his clothes even if he wouldn't know what to do in a fight.

Bud must have been convinced of something because he said, "Maybe I'll need some help. Even split. How about it?"

"We'll see," Mike said. He wanted to play it safe. He didn't think he could count on Cuddles and Danny if he tried to tip them off. They were both crazy drunk, and would probably think he was lying and gang up on him with their old friend Bud.

Bud and Mike stood there ready to fight if necessary but very reluctant to get down to it. Just then Danny and Cuddles came back with a taxi driver and they all piled into the cab. "Drive uptown," Bud said. They drove up Third Avenue and crossed Forty-second. That much Mike could tell. Somewhere in the upper Forties Bud told the driver to stop. Cuddles paid the driver off.

As Mike got out of the cab, Bud bumped into him and roughed him up. "This guy's up to something," Bud said, looking to the others for support.

Mike knotted himself together, twitched his shoulder without much hope, snorted through his nose like a fighter, and waited for something to happen. He and Bud faced each other warily, waiting for Danny and Cuddles to make a move. "All right, all right," Cuddles said. "The beer's inside." It was all over.

They went into the bar arm in arm. The bartender didn't want anything to do with them they were so drunk, but he gave them beer to prevent a fight.

It was only a couple of beers before Danny got sick. As Mike got up to take him out for air, Bud winked at him. Mike nodded secretly.

This of course was just what Mike had been waiting for, but by the time he got Danny outside he was no good for anything but to hang over a little rail around a freight elevator. All the while Danny was being sick, Mike was repeating, "This guy Bud is out to roll you. He's after your money. He wanted me to help him."

And all the while Danny kept on shaking his head and vomiting and not understanding at all. Then he straightened up and said, "Oh he is, is he?"

Mike had just got his work in in time because the others were coming out of the bar. "Here they come now," Mike said. "Tell

Cuddles and let's make an end to this." Danny nodded with his face all closed together.

"How do you feel, Danny?" Cuddles said.

"Better," Danny said.

"I want to talk to you for a minute," Cuddles said.

"Good," Danny said.

Bud and Mike stood there together for a minute while Danny and Cuddles whispered in the shadows. "Is he ready?" Bud said.

"He's ready all right," Mike said, well pleased with the hidden meaning of what he said. He looked at Bud with hate that he took little trouble to hide.

Danny and Cuddles were coming back. Mike raised his eyebrow to Danny. Danny nodded curtly and came over and stood beside him, slipping his arm around his shoulder. Suddenly Danny was behind him, holding his arms while Cuddles and Bud punched him in the face.

At first Mike was too shocked to protect his face. Then he began to buck and writhe to get rid of Danny. He lashed back with his head at Danny's face until Danny tucked his head down close. All the while the other two kept beating at his head and shoulders although by then he was much harder to hit accurately. He horsed Danny over to the corner of the building and tried to beat him off against the sharp edge of the bricks. After one particularly brutal lunge in which he was sure he caught Danny's head between his back and the bricks, he was able to break loose. But he went stumbling off balance across the sidewalk into two screaming women. Cuddles ran after him all the way and smashed his fist into the back of his neck before he could straighten. That sent him flat on his face. He got up as far as his hands and knees. Danny was beside him with half of his face a bloody mass. Danny kicked at his ribs but it didn't stop him and he kept coming up. But Bud was behind him and kicked in between his legs.

That was all.

He lay there puking but nothing mattered. There was a lot of running. There were police whistles. But nothing mattered. He had a vague idea that this would be useful in explaining why he hadn't got back to work that afternoon, but not even that mattered.

Why I Play Rugby

The first time I saw Rugby played was in Oxford in the spring of 1959. I was slogging along a deep and dirty lane, admiring the trees, admiring the hedgerow, admiring even the rain—I think I would have been disappointed if the sun had been shining when I took my first walk through the English countryside. It was a rare moment of content. I had just seen a chaffinch. I was pleased with my stout English boots and my surplus poncho. I had even forgotten my disappointment at arriving in England too late for the Rugby season.

Although I felt myself to be a solitary figure in a landscape, I was not surprised to see a football sailing over the hedge and dropping toward me. Instinctively I held out my hands and the football settled into the basket made by my poncho. It was a football I was very glad to see, fat and ungainly like the footballs of my childhood. I worked my hands free and fondled it. Oh, it was a football.

My friend Patrick, who discovered Rugby here in the cornfields, says Rugby is a very physical game and that he plays it to unburden himself of those blows which, according to Robert Frost (Patrick says), a life of self-control requires that we spare to strike for the common good. And there must be a lot in that. All I have to do is feel that lovely football and I think of the endless games of my childhood and the twin ecstasies of smashing and being smashed, of those moments when the whole world hangs in a crunching equilibrium. And I see Patrick's face as he comes off the field after the first half. His hair and beard stand out in a ring, and his face gleams like a monstrance at the moment of truth. I hand him a section of an orange. "He's very large," I say, referring to the opposing prop. "But docile," Patrick says. "Just so," I say deferentially—Patrick is only in his middle twenties but he is a hero, a genuine Viking in spite of his Irish name. If he stepped ashore on the coast of England, the old church bells would know him and would quake in their belfries and the countryside would turn out to repel him. His face is streaming with sweat and light. His eye roves constantly as if searching out larger, less docile props. He is himself small for a prop, five foot ten, say, and a hundred ninety pounds, and his present opponent is six inches and fifty pounds bigger. "I can do what I want with him," Patrick is saying. "When I saw his size I knew I would have to be firm with him from the start." Patrick eyes a field full of varsity football players (American style) doing calisthenics across the street. "Nothing to get him angry, of course. Nothing crude. I wasn't going to swing on his beard, mind you. Can you imagine what he would be if he ever got fired up? And I wasn't about to pluck out a handful of hair from his armpit. You know all that sort of thing." I really don't, never having been a prop, but Patrick is very considerate—I'm weighing *chivalrous* against him. He sucks his orange and measures the football team. "I'd pull their beards," he says. "If they had any," I say. "So much the worse for them," he says. I don't care to pursue that line of thought. The mysteries of the scrum are best left alone. "What friendly hint did you give your large friend?" I say at last. "In the first two scrums," Patrick says, "instead of locking shoulders with him, as he has every right to expect, I met him with my skull between his eyes. He got the message." Patrick throws down his orange skin and runs out onto the field. He waves his arms like windmills and throws himself fiercely down, bounds up, stamps out a terrible message on the earth. All about my feet the brilliant spring grass is littered violent orange. Patrick locks in for the first scrum. His head disappears. His thigh muscles stand out. The strain builds up. His shorts split up the back. His ass gleams forth. Everyone cheers. Toward the end of the match, while Patrick is lying unconscious on the sidelines, a member of the B squad donates his shorts, which are slipped onto Patrick so he can rage back into action at the first signs of life.

I climbed up out of the lane and went through the hedge by a kissing gate and found myself at the edge of a sports ground. A game was in progress. I walked into the grounds unmolested, fondling the ball, my fingers remembering its slippery curves, my arms and legs remembering strength and speed. I could have sprung upstairs two at a time if there had been stairs. The smell of bruised grass and mud. The lovely tiredness of muscles. Aches and bruises just beginning gently to assert themselves. A player, hotly pursued, pivoted and kicked the ball over a hedge into the motorway. "Oh, well kicked," a man near me said. He took my ball and threw it onto the field. "Good man," his friend said and clapped him on the back, nearly falling off his crutches in his enthusiasm. There seemed to be only the three of us watching. "Got to keep them at it," the first man said. His speech was decidedly mushy, and I noticed now that he had no front teeth and that his upper lip was stitched like a baseball. "Jolly good," the man on crutches said, although I have no witnesses to it. "I'll be glad when I'm too old to play," Mushmouth said. "It's not much longer for either of us," the other said. A player, this time on the other team, pivoted and kicked the ball into the motorway. "Oh, well kicked," my companions said. "Oh, jolly good."

The rain was blowing in gray sheets across the pitch. I opened my flask under my poncho and pulled in my head like a turtle going into retirement. I suppose I must have looked remarkably like a man pretending not to be taking a drink under a poncho, but I had no information about right conduct at a Rugby match. "I'm sorry," I said when I reappeared and saw the other two staring into my shell. "Perhaps you would care—" I said. They boarded me at once. "Jolly good," one said. "Well drunk," the other said. We finished it off, turn and turn about scrupulously. Brandy, then, was definitely acceptable at a Rugby match—at least in bad weather.

In the Britannia down in back of Swiss Cottage—it was my local on one of my stays in London—on a Saturday morning—I can't remember why I happened to be in there, because drinking in the morning is not ordinarily my thing, but then, I guess you travel in order to be relieved of your thing—or something—and a couple of

pints in your local at lunchtime really isn't drinking at all. The pub
XV were in there, shouting and singing as usual—you should hear
them on a Sunday night when they come in straight from a match.
You'd think they had driven the Romans off the wall and chased
them all the way to London. On that Saturday they were all of them
going down to Twickenham and were even more inflamed than
usual. I had a suspicion that they did not intend to visit the shrine of
Alexander Pope, but it was Pope who persisted in coming into mind
at each mention of Twickenham. I kept quiet and listened and
sipped my Guinness, laying down in the glass a lovely tight series of
foam rings that would have done credit to the most frugal old Irishman in the frugal west country. Twickenham, I eventually gathered,
was Yankee Stadium. And it was Cooperstown. And it was the
World Series. Revenge was the theme. Revenge against France, last
year's super-champion. The XV must have liked the color of my
Guinness or the cunning of my silence, because, after offering a
spare ticket to everyone in the place, they asked if I'd go with them.
They must have observed by then that I never had anything in particular to do.

Until that Saturday I had believed that the only place in London
you could drink all day was Lord's Cricket Ground—there are many
interesting things to learn in London. It was a ridiculously cheap
ticket. Six shillings perhaps. I stood in the sun on the terrace with
the heavy bark of ENG-LAND in one ear and in the other the light,
quick chant *Allez la France, allez la France, allez.* It was marvelous
being there, packed in shoulder to shoulder. The play was like the
shouts, strength against quickness, but it was all very beautiful, fluid
and powerful. Strength won handsomely that day, but I remember
chiefly a white-haired man on the England side—my friend Patrick
tells me that a prop doesn't mature until after thirty—and the drifts
of wine bottles on the terraces at the end of the match. The sun, the
crowd, the flowing play, and a chanticleer crowing all afternoon on
someone's shoulder down in front of us. Later I read that the white-
haired man was only in his twenties, but the news came too late, the
picture was set by then.

Patrick tells me that he is planning to write a book about Rugby.

From what I can gather, it is to be about everything in the game and out of it that makes him a player. He's going to call it WHY I PLAY RUGBY, but he wants to wait until he is at least fifty before he begins. He hopes to attain wisdom, he says.

The rain was blowing gray along the sides of Helvellyn. Just above my head, it seemed, the white clouds were flowing over the saddle toward Patterdale. But as I came over a little rise I saw ahead of me yet another small valley with the trail going up on the other side, all but obliterated by rock slides. I had already given up the idea of reaching the top and was contenting myself with simply finding the pass and the tarn and going down to the highway on the other side. Somehow my imagination had been caught by the picture of Wordsworth saying what was to be his last goodbye to his brother near the tarn. That would satisfy me. I crossed the valley and climbed over the rocks along what remained of the old pack-horse trail. Patches of fog—clouds, should I say?—enveloped me briefly. It was very cold. Very silent. Very lonely. The wind was terrific. It would be easy to lose the trail in the fog. A fall would be nasty. However, there were cairns every few yards to keep me honest, so I advanced from cairn to cairn in the clearer moments. And after a scramble on hands and knees, I stood beside a cairn like all the others and waited for a lucid moment. When it came, I saw that this time the horizon had not skulked off a few more yards but that below me the tarn lay in a pocket and beyond that endless space.

The tarn, I saw as I walked beside it, was streaked with foam, long thin white lines from end to end. The wind was battering my body. My legs trembled. If I hadn't been so hungry, I think I might well have lain down and died on the spot. As it was, I went on as best I could. So absorbed was I in my physical self that I failed to observe a file of figures trotting toward me. They came into focus very close at hand, and I cringed against a rock to let them pass. The leader, I saw, carried a football. It was, in fact, a Rugby club, dressed as if for a match, running through the pass, silent and tireless as Indians. As I crossed the outlet to the tarn, the wind blew me off the stepping-stones into ankle-deep water, and I slogged on down the easy descent with my shoes full of water and my heart full of despair. It was only

when I found a pub and sat down that I thought again of Wordsworth, of the foam-streaked tarn, and of the low white clouds, the
slanting gray rain, the endless space and the quiet.

It's a sensation of power, Patrick says. A moment when you can
feel the entire power of the pack focusing in your hips and thighs,
and you are ready to launch yourself, to grapple—and you feel a
vague dissatisfaction that your opponent is merely mortal, for you
know you are yourself much more. It must be, he says, to witness
that moment that the Rugby girls come out—Rugger-huggers he
calls them and laughs at them but acknowledges that they are his
real witnesses. And perhaps, he continues, that is also why many
wives cannot come out to watch, not, as one might suppose, for fear
of seeing their husbands broken up on the field but for fear of seeing
them in glory, a naked display of what should be their secret joy, but
what is, in fact, their secret grief. Quite probably there are many
wives who know they will never have from their husbands what the
husbands make a public display of time after effortless time on a
Saturday afternoon. That's what Patrick talks like and that's where,
in his idiom, his head is. I think he'll write a marvelous book about
Rugby. Or it may be a poem-novel like Wordsworth's *Prelude:* The
Growth of a Poet's Mind or A Rugby Player Finds Out Where His
Head Is At.

When we got to the party, the visiting side was already puking on
the lawn. "Jesus," Patrick said, "who brought them along?" This
was not the Rugby party but quite a different one, intended, at least,
to be very sedate. Patrick and I had left the Rugby party in full blast,
we thought. It was being held in an abandoned garage that made me
think of the St. Valentine's Day Massacre. The place was shaped
like a shoebox, all concrete, nothing to break, the floor caked with
grease and a faint smell of hot metal still in the air. Kegs of beer
were scattered around strategically, but there was nothing else in the
box except what I took to be two enormous white refrigerators set
down very much in the way. When the visiting team tipped one over
with our scrum half inside, it became quite clear that they were portable toilets. There threatened to be some unpleasantness for a while,
but our side was still sober enough to understand that you might very

well run up a lopsided score against those monsters, but you would do very well not to make too much of an upset toilet in an abandoned garage. They were really big. They had come over from Indianapolis, and Patrick said they looked to him like the machines that had failed to qualify for the 500.

So when we found them heaving up their guts on the lawn we were not particularly pleased. But gradually we got them stacked in the back of their van—it was a panel truck. Probably some of them had a rock group, because the van was painted in wild colors and patterns and I made out something I took to read The Vroom. About this time, a wife appeared and jumped into the back of the van and began stomping and kicking about very urgently as if to work the ball loose. Eventually she came out with the keys and scuttled around the van, giving us a dirty look as she went, and got in and drove them all off.

After that, Patrick and I, although conscious of having behaved very well, were somehow not at ease at that party, so we went back to the garage. As we went in, we held out our hands to show the foot-balls stamped on our palms—there had been a historic fight at a party where some visiting Blacks were stamped on their palms while everyone else was being stamped on the back of their hands. Of course, the ink would show up only on the Blacks' palms, but they claimed discrimination and could be satisfied only by being beaten insensible. It took three weeks of debate and other persuasion for the club to adopt a rule that everyone should be stamped on the palm forevermore. So we showed our palms but there was no one there to see them.

I thought at first that the Massacre had been reenacted. But, of course, it was only the beer. "It's a massacre," Patrick said. We checked the bodies. All seemed in good shape. We checked the toi-lets, which were both on their sides. There was a girl asleep in the Ladies. I couldn't cope, so I gagged and closed the door. In a dark corner in the back I found a girl sitting on a beer keg with her feet tucked up out of the mess. "I knew someone would find me," she said. "I knew some prop would carry me out of here." She held out her arms toward us. "I'm sorry," Patrick said, "my wife doesn't approve of my carrying girls anywhere, period." He disappeared, pouf. "Let's get the hell out of here and go find a beer," I said. I picked her up. "You're so strong," she said. My knees were buckling, and if the garage had been ten feet longer, I'd never have made it, but as it was I set her down outside the door. I was able to control my breath and my trembling muscles, but I didn't yet trust myself to speak, so I began walking off blindly to the left with my hand firmly on her arm. "My car is this way," she said, kneading my biceps and turning me around. It was not what you would call a meaningful relationship, but it was very pleasant. I noticed that when we got to her place, I went up the stairs two at a time on the balls of my feet.

Once my flask was empty I began to feel the cold. Crutches and Mushmouth had gone all huddled and glum. They were no longer making an effort to follow the action up and down the sidelines. Water was getting inside my poncho now. My feet were either cold or wet—or both—but I was afraid it might be unsporting to go away. I looked toward the clubhouse at the end of the pitch and saw that it was now lighted. People were gathered at the windows drinking beer and watching the game. It seemed somehow very civilized. "Lucky sods," Crutches said. "We'll have our turn," Mushmouth said. "Five more years of being keen," Crutches said. "Five at the outside," Mushmouth said. "Being keen is hell," Crutches said. "Bloody hell," I said. They looked at me as if they had forgotten all about me. "But it pays off," Crutches said. "They watch," Mushmouth said. "Oh, well caught," he said. "Jolly good," Crutches said. I glanced toward the clubhouse but no one seemed to be paying much attention to anything outside.

Patrick was terrific but the snow was also terrific. Out on the field the players faded in and out like TV ghosts, and the electric orange and blue hoops of their jerserys were muted to pastels even at close range. It was a very impressionistic scene. I kept getting an image of Canterbury cathedral manifesting itself out of just such a storm at the end of a three-day mid-April walk from London.

It was a very sloppy match and very fierce. Patrick was raging up and down the field being firm. There was one time he tackled four runners one after another, flinging them down as they passed off and then collaring the receiver almost at the same time. He was a one-man pack. Nobody was saving anything that day, because it was the last match until spring, but he was letting it all go as if he planned to hibernate. Then they got him on a little up-and-under kick that dropped right into his hands. They were all around him but he broke two tackles and gave someone time to get into position to take his pass. He passed off and the play started to flow away from him, and then, very high and very late, he caught a great flying sprawling tackle. When he went down it was clear he wouldn't get up, not even Patrick. There was a terrific fight back and forth across him. Everyone on both sides was in on it. The referee was blowing his whistle like mad. The B teams were charging onto the field. I ran out along with the other two or three spectators. And then it stopped. We just stood and looked at the snow reddening around Patrick's head.

The referee looked at his watch. "Such another outbreak," he said, "and I shall abandon the match." He held the ball firmly under his arm as if he were ready to go home with it. He sent off the player who had hit Patrick, as was only right. Even I had seen that elbow come down like a club. The rest of us carried Patrick off, and even before we had crossed the touch line the game was raging again.

Patrick was obviously a hospital case. Not only had he lost some teeth but his jaw was almost certainly broken. He was showing no signs of coming around, so we began casting about for someone with a car. I was the logical one, but I made a point of never bringing my car. It gave me a good excuse to catch a ride with Patrick or somebody after the match and stop in with the players for a beer. There was a girl, however, who volunteered to drive. I said I'd go along.

Now I had noticed this girl, and I flattered myself she had noticed me. Well, she wasn't all that girlish. What — thirty — give or take a couple of years. Anyway, at the half I was measuring out a hot toddy from my thermos for Patrick and another for myself. We had taken refuge in a corner of the tennis courts where a practice wall broke the wind. I offered her a drink too. She was glad to have it. She turned out to be from New Zealand. None of your regular Ruggerhuggers but a true aficionada, a little homesick. She had a brother who had been an All Black. While she was wrapping her fingers around my cup and warming them and her nose at the same time, I was bouncing a golf ball on the court. It had been lying in the corner in some leaves, lost no doubt by someone practicing on the field. I was bouncing and talking and very well pleased with myself. She was nice. She was interested. I had real hopes. But I got carried away and bounced carelessly. The ball hopped toward her. She made a motion to catch it and it landed in her cup. The toddy splashed on her hands and her coat. She was marvelous about it but I felt like a fool. Patrick thought it was very funny.

So it was this girl who volunteered to drive Patrick to the hospital and who looked toward me when someone was needed to go with her. We stuffed Patrick into her car and I got in. In two minutes she had the car at right angles to the road. The front wheels were up on the crown of the road, and the back wheels were in the ditch. I got out and tried pushing but with no luck at all. I went and got the B team and we formed in back of the car. I put my shoulder to the trunk. I felt the hard bodies of men on either side of me. I felt hands on my back, a shoulder under my butt. The entire power of the pack was focused in my hips and thighs as the car launched itself onto the road. And something went pop in my groin. She left both of us at the hospital.

The losing team ran off the field toward the clubhouse. I wanted to shout "Bad show," but my companions, Crutches and Mushmouth, were watching benignly, so I didn't presume. The losers suddenly stopped and formed a line on either side of the clubhouse door and applauded as the winners sauntered past them. "Good show," Mushmouth said. He and Crutches made their way slowly toward the clubhouse. The losers collapsed their lines and jostled on in.

The first time I saw Rugby I was already far too old to play.

In Northumberland Once

It was always an egg pan. As he moved from hostel to hostel, it was always an egg pan—except when someone had burned the porridge. He sometimes wondered if there was a secret mark on his card that said EGG PAN. He felt like the chorus girl who found herself being seduced in every town by the clarinet player in the local band—it was always a clarinet player. In that case, there really was a secret mark on the music that went along with the show. There was no mystery about it at all. He examined his card but could learn nothing. To be on the safe side, however, he added more stains at random, dots and pen scratches front and back, and tore off two additional corners. He still got the egg pan. His alternative theory was that any man his age who didn't right off say "Shove the egg pan" could be counted on to stay with it until it was really clean. Not like those kids.

He turned now to the pan. It was crusted with yellow. He always saved it for last, hating to put the other pans into the nasty water it left.

"Cold water for egg pans," his wife always said.

He ran the water as hot as he could stand and attacked the pan with his fingernails, his secret weapon.

It wasn't bad once he got down to it. He rinsed his hands
and washed the yellow high-water marks off his forearms
and left the pan, with all the others, out for inspection.

> "Dishwasher
> puts dishes
> away," his
> wife said.

"Not everywhere," he said. "Not here."

> "Everywhere,"
> she said.
> "There are no
> exceptions."

He went to the bunk room and picked up his pack and
then to the office for his card. "Pans done?" the warden
said.

"Of course," he said. He had been three nights at this
hostel, and he knew the pans had been checked.

"Right," the warden said and gave him his card. "Have a
good day."

"Right," he said.

> "Put away the
> pans," his
> wife said.

He stepped out into the street, to the row of stone cot-
tages, to the billowing hills behind them, brown, russet, and
dun, very rich. The air was clear. He seemed to be at the
edge of a vast plateau, high, very high.

> "Mean altitude," his
> wife said, "at or near
> the six-hundred-foot
> contour line."

The pub was open, he noticed, so he just stepped in. The
barmaid was standing at attention behind the pulls. He
hadn't intended to have anything, but he automatically ordered a pint of bitter. "And how far is it to Bamburgh?" he
said.

"Bamburgh?" the barmaid said. "Sam, how far is it to Bamburgh?"

"Bamburgh?" a man said. Mason turned. The man was slouched in a dark corner, admiring a full pint on the table before him.

"Yes," Mason said. "I want to see Bamburgh Castle."

The first known
king was Ida (547),
who ruled at
Bamburgh for
twelve years
and built
Bamburgh Castle,
the Arthurian
Joyous Garde,
Lancelot's Castle.

"Oh, castles," the barmaid said. "Have you seen the castle at Newcastle?"

"Oh yes," Mason said. "It's very fine."

"Perhaps you are thinking of Bedlington," the man said.

"There's no castle at Bedlington," the barmaid said.

"Or Bellingham. It's small but nice."

"What would he want at Bellingham?"

"Bamburgh," Mason said.

"There's a lovely castle at Alnwich," the barmaid said.

"Oh yes," the man said. "We're very proud of it."

"Or Warkworth," the barmaid said. "How about Warkworth, Sam?"

"Oh, very good," the man said. "Harry Percy's house."

The Hotspur of
the North: he
that kills me
some six or seven
dozen of Scots
at a breakfast,
washes his hands,
and says to his

wife, "Fie upon
this quiet life—
I want work."

"You tempt me," Mason said.

"I'll Hotspur you,"
his wife said.

"Bamburgh, you say?" the man said. "That will be forty
or fifty miles from here."

"Oh, more," the barmaid said. "Much more. It's ever so
far."

Ida was followed
by four of his sons
in succession:
Glappa (559-560),
Adda (560-568),
Aethelric (568-572),
and Theodoric (572-579).
Nothing is known of
the first three except
their names.

"Barely forty," the man said.

Ida's fourth son
is said to have
been beseiged in
Lindisfarne (Holy
Island) by the Welsh.

Mason had checked his map the night before and figured
it at forty-five to fifty. "Or the Wall," he said. "How far is it
to the Wall?"

"Why would you want to go to Wall?" the barmaid said.
"There's no castle there."

"No," the man said. "Nor nothing much else."

"A nice enough town—in a small way, of course," the
barmaid said.

"Very nice," the man said. "Quiet."

"They're making
a fool of you,"
his wife said.

Mason was prepared for this. He had observed the town
of Wall on his map. It was actually near where he wanted to
go. "No, no." He laughed, pretending he had been taken in.
"I meant the Roman Wall, Hadrian's Wall, the Picts'
Wall."

The Wall was begun
by Hadrian (c. 122 A.D.)
and finished by
Aulus Platorius Nepos.
It was rebuilt of
stone by Septimius
Severus (c. 208).

"Far," the barmaid said, "if you're going to go by the way
of Wall."

"All of thirty-five miles," the man said.

"More," the barmaid said. "More than that."

Mason tried not to smile. He was, in fact, going by way of
Wall. His information was that Housesteads was the best
place to get at the Wall.

Borcovicus
(Housesteads)
was one of the
principle forts
on the Wall. Its
layout as now
excavated is typical
and instructive.

"I must be off," he said, "if I'm going to walk on the Wall
at all. I must be in London tomorrow night."

"Bad luck," the barmaid said.

"But I'd like to leave a pint for the warden when he looks
in tonight. He'll drink a pint, I suppose."

"He's been known to," the barmaid said.

"You're going to walk on the Wall?" the man said.

"I hope so," Mason said. He counted the money out on the bar.

> "Willie Ball
> walked on the
> wall," he sang,
> and Willie Ball
> hit him in the
> stomach.

"Thank you," the barmaid said. "I'll see that he gets it."

> He hit Willie Ball
> in the mouth.

"Thank you," Mason said. He had every confidence in her, standing there at attention behind the pulls. "Good morning." He included the man in the corner slouched over his full pint, but he got no reply from either. He went out of the pub, out of the village, and he was alone on the highway.

Aethelfrith (593-616)
was defeated and
killed in battle by
Edwin, whose place
he had usurped.

> Or not quite alone. As he approached the intersection of the village road with the main route, he saw two figures resting on the grassy bank. A boy and a girl. The girl was wearing a very short skirt. Hitchhikers, then. Not really serious. She was also crying.

At the death of
Edwin (633), the
kingdom was
divided, and
both kings were
killed by
Caedwalla, king
of the Welsh, in
the following year.

When she became aware of him, she flopped over and hid her face. The boy continued to stare ahead of him, hugging his knees and rocking. It was up to Mason to find out which way they were going and allow them first ride. "Are you waiting for a ride?" he said. The boy didn't answer. They were clearly Americans, so it couldn't be language. "Which way are you going?" He aimed this at the girl's back.

"That's right," his wife said. "Now drop on one knee to get a good look up her skirt—don't you dare. Bastard."

"Don't know," the boy said. "I think we've had it."

"Anything I can do?"

"You don't happen to have a hot bath about you?"

"I'm afraid not," Mason said. "How about a cigarette?" The boy took two but only held them.

"Next he'll be asking for a square meal and a round bed," the girl said without turning over.

"Goddamn it," his wife said. "I'm not tired. I'm not hungry. And I haven't got my period."

"It's too many nights in the open," the boy said. "We were too late for the hostel again last night."

"Too goddamn much of everything," the girl said.

"OK, so we'll start back," the boy said.

"I don't want to start back," the girl said. The boy and Mason looked at each other and shrugged. Mason offered him a chocolate bar. Now he had the cigarettes in one hand and the chocolate in the other. They both looked at the girl.

"Enough of that,"
his wife said. "I'll
not have another
Margot, and I
don't care how
many years ago
that was. It
was our honeymoon,
and you looked
at her legs.

"Perhaps some rest—" Mason said.
"Fuck," the girl said.

"That doesn't
fix a thing,"
his wife said.

The boy and Mason made deprecating gestures to each
other. The boy dropped a cigarette and picked it up again.
"Thanks," he said. Mason continued along the highway.

Coelwulf (731)
was deposed and
forced to become
a monk.

He walked to the top of a rise where he could easily be
seen. He looked about him. The country was magnificent,
wide-spread and rolling, very empty. "*Esperance,*" he said,
"and Percy."

Aethelstan defeated
Norwegians, Scots,
and the rightful heir
at Brunanburgh (937):

They left behind them   in charge of the bodies
the black-coated raven   ready to ravage,
horn-billed and greedy,   and the grey-coated
eagle, him with the white tail,   wheeling for plunder,

grimmest of war thanes,   and that grey goer,
wolf of the wold,   war grave of heroes.

Nothing was moving on the road, so he slipped off his
pack and sat on a stone wall. Giving away the chocolate bar
had made him hungry for chocolate, so he ate half a bar,
early elevenses. Young rams were banging skulls in the
field.

> And he grabbed
> Willie Ball, and
> Willie Ball
> grabbed him.
> And they at it
> and fought, as
> the story says.

A car stopped to offer him a ride, but really to ask directions. It was going the wrong way anyway. For a moment he
was tempted but only for a moment. With his map in his
hand he gave a learned discourse on highway conditions and
the nature of local pubs. He'd been through all that.

Oswulf was murdered
by his followers (759).

When he was alone again, he climbed over the stone wall
into the field with the sheep. He looked all around carefully
and pissed against the wall.

> "Nasty," his
> wife said.

The young rams took a long look at him and went back to
their work.

> They knocked
> the hard ground
> into soft and
> the soft ground
> into hard, the

rocks into
spring wells
and the spring
wells into
rocks.

It was always a mistake to have a pint in the morning. What
if he got a ride?

His first ride took him as far as Corbridge. It wasn't a
long ride, but it came quickly and the day was young. "I can
take you as far as Corbridge," the man said.

Aethelred was
murdered at
Corbridge (796).

"Oh, fine," Mason said. "That's a big help." He hadn't
really sorted out all the towns along the route, but any move
was a good move.

"Where are you going?" the man said.

"I hope to get to Housesteads to look at the Roman
stuff."

"Oh, Roman," the man said. "Corbridge is your place.
Not one but two Roman forts. Very fine. Hunnum and Cor-
stopitum."

"How about the Wall?" Mason said.

"Not much around here, I must admit," the man said.
"But if you like churches—"

"Oh yes," Mason said. "Very much."

"There's a fine old church. Saxon, they say. Long and
short work, that sort of thing. I expect that's where you'll
find the Wall—right in the church, that is. Roman stone."

"Two birds with one stone," Mason said.

"A bird in the
hand," his wife said.

But when he got out at Corbridge, he didn't look at the church or the forts. If he was stuck here, he could make do with them, but he had really committed himself to the Wall.

> Willie Ball was
> stronger than he
> ever thought.
> There must be
> something to all
> that training-camp
> stuff, all that road
> work, lifting weights.

His next ride was to Hexam. He could have gone all the way to Carlisle, but his road turned north now. The ride was even shorter than the first, but it came quickly.

Oswald ruled
twenty-seven days
and was forced to
become a monk (796).

The ride was with a doctor's wife. She didn't say why she was going to Carlisle or where the doctor was, but Mason could smell his medicine and his cigars.

> "Two of a kind,"
> his wife said.
> "Thumbing rides with
> women, giving rides
> to men."

"You mustn't miss the Abbey," she said.

"Oh no," Mason said. "I've read about it."

"It's practically a What's What of church architecture," she said.

"I hope I have time for it," Mason said. "I've got to get on to the Wall at Housesteads."

There must be
something to
that farmboy
stuff, all that
loading hay,
lifting grain bags.

"Oh, Roman work," she said. "The Abbey is full of Roman capitals and cornices. Other things as well."

"Probably part of the Wall, too, " Mason said. "Maybe I needn't go to all that trouble."

"Surely part of the Wall," she said. "And a very special inscription. Actually it's a stone from which an inscription was erased."

"Oh?" he said.

"Oh yes," she said. "It wasn't enough for the Emperor Caracalla to murder his brother, but he wanted to obliterate him completely and ordered his name to be rubbed out all over the empire. Isn't that terrible?"

"Yes," Mason said. "Terrible."

With a quick
twist and buck
he got free of
Willie Ball and
stood up again.

It was indeed sufficiently terrible. To have your name rubbed out all over the world. To have it hunted out on the remote borders of darkest Britain and erased from stone. "Perhaps you have sons?" he said, rather to his own surprise.

"Yes," she said, "nine and seven."

"Oh, very good," he said.

"Yes," she said. "I hope so." She looked stricken as she let him out but rallied—or attempted to. "Don't forget the Abbey," she said.

"No," he said. "Of course not."

"Hypocrite," his
wife said.

He thought of taking a quick look at the Abbey, but as he
was standing by the road making up his mind, he got
another ride.

Ella, defeated
in battle, was
treacherously
murdered by his
followers (866).

"Where are you going?" the man said.

"Housesteads to look at the Wall," Mason said.

"Ah, yes," the man said. "Hadrian and all that."

"Right," Mason said.

"Picts and Scots and the Pax Romana," the man said.
His car was good and he was casually dressed as if for an
evening in a fashionable pub in Hampstead.

Mason laughed. It was already a little wearing.

"I might just go look at the Wall," the man said. "Never
have, you know. Shameful."

"Isn't that just the way?" Mason said doggedly. "Live
right around it and never see it."

"Oh, I don't live here," the man said. "I'm on holiday."

"Oh," Mason said.

"The Wall," the man said. "Yes, I believe I will."

"Willie Ball is
slow coming out.
And Dempsey is
waiting in the
center of the ring."

"It would be very convenient," Mason said.

"I'd like the company," the man said. "What do you say
to lunch?"

"Why not?" Mason said. He had lots of time now.

Dempsey goes
after that eye
again. He misses
but keeps boring
in, pouring it on.
The cut is opened."

"I know an inn near Wall," the man said. "Or Chollerford, perhaps?"

"I really can't choose," Mason said.

"Chollerford, then. It will be good time for lunch."

Healfdene was
killed in Ireland
after he had been
expelled from his
country and lost
his reason as a
punishment for his
misdeeds (877).

"Sounds good to me," Mason said.

"Where are you going after the Wall?"

"I'm not sure. I have to be in London tomorrow night."

"Tell you what," the man said. "If things work out, why
don't you come back with me to Hexam. That's my base.
I've got a fine place there and can put you up easily. Drive
you to Newcastle in the morning for your train."

"Blood is everywhere.
And the referee stops
it. It's all over.
And still champion."

"That sounds like a lot of trouble," Mason said.

"Not at all. Glad to do it. Holiday sort of thing."

In Georgia once.
Hitchhiking.
There was something
wrong with the drink.
("Aha," his wife said.)

"I couldn't impose," Mason said.
"Not a bit of it," the man said.
"I'm afraid—"
"My pleasure."

Long ago, in
Athens, Georgia.
In the salesman's
room. His legs wouldn't
work. ("Aha," his
wife said.)

"I've really got to get back," Mason said.
"Married?" the man said.
"Divorced," Mason said. Again he was surprised. That
wasn't the kind of thing he went around telling people.
"Then what's the hurry? Girl friend?"
"No, no. Nothing like that."

But that wasn't
the way. You
didn't hit
Willie Ball on
his sty. It was
one of the rules.

"Then it's settled."
"I couldn't think of it," Mason said.
"Nothing at all. My pleasure."

Another rule
was that he
didn't get hit
himself on his
cold sore.

"That's what I'm afraid of," Mason said. "No offense."
"No, no, none at all."

Willie Ball was
very strong. He
hit very hard.
Wham. On the
nose. A mouthful
of blood.

"But I think we'd better understand each other," Mason
said.

In Athens,
Georgia, in the
salesman's bed
he looked all
night at cars
driving away down
a very long street.

"Oh, by all means," the man said. "Let us understand
each other."
"I think we'd better understand just what is involved."
"I think you know," the man said.

He hit Willie
Ball on the sty,
and Willie Ball
ran home crying.
("Bastard," his
wife said. "So
that's it.")

"I think I do," Mason said. "And it's no go. No offense."

"Oh, no. But if it's all the same to you, I'd just as soon you got out here. No offense. Holidays, you know."

"None at all," Mason said. He reached around for his pack and was ready when the car stopped. The driver whipped it around and headed back toward Hexam very fast.

Guthred, a slave,
became king at the
command of St.
Cuthbert, who
appeared in a dream
to Eadred, the abbot
of Carlisle (883).

Now Mason was late again, so he took up a serious position at the side of the road. Not only was he late but he might be stranded as well. He couldn't remember seeing any cars since they left Hexam. He could walk back all right, but he couldn't hope to walk on. He was also hungry, so he ate the rest of his chocolate and an apple he had bought the day before.

He looked after
Willie Ball.
His friends
looked at him.
Nobody picked
up his coat.

The first car that came along stopped for him. Actually it was a van. "I'm going as far as Bellingham," the man said. "Will that help?"

"Anything will help," Mason said. "I'm going to Housesteads."

"Bad luck," the man said. "But I'll drop you at Choller-ford at your turning."

"That's fine," Mason said. Perhaps in a pinch he could

walk from Chollerford. He had figured the distance at about ten miles.

"I'll be stopping at Wall to make a delivery," the man said. "But I'll only be a minute."

"Be my guest," Mason said.

The man looked startled. Then laughed. "Going to see the Wall?" he said.

"I didn't mean to," he said. ("A likely story," his wife said.) But they all turned and went into Maud Nutter's candy store. He could hear their pennies clicking against the pegs in the slot machine.

"Right," Mason said.

"Wish I could go with you," the man said. "But it's ten miles out of my way, and I'm late already."

Mason almost lost courage as the driver turned abruptly and plunged through a narrow gap in a high stone wall. They were in a small village around a green.

"Wall," the man said.

There was a shout. Someone must have won. "All right," Maud said bitterly. "I see it."

The stop at Wall was very short. So was the ride to Chollerford. The new road was clearly less traveled than the last one, and after buying chocolate, apples, biscuits, and two bottles of Guinness, he set out walking with only an occasional glance over his shoulder.

Anlaf Godfreyson
died on a raid
into the south of
Scotland (942).

He walked all the way. In the first hour he waved to the people on the tourist buses. They were the ones moving, but they waved as if he were an engineer on a train. He gave up all hope of supper at the hostel. During the second hour he walked with his head down. "The Wall," he said to himself. "The Wall." He gave up sleeping in the hostel that night. At least he knew he ought to give it up. There was no way he could get back before it closed.

He had once won
a quarter. Maud
wouldn't let him
spend it all at
once on candy but
gave him three
cents a day until
it was gone.

He was very tired when he got to Housesteads. A tour bus was just pulling away, and the place was deserted. He stood for a moment and looked up the slope. It was really here. He was here.

Eric Bloodaxe, exiled
king of Norway, took
the throne (950).

He advanced slowly, not because he was tired. He had forgotten that. His pack was nothing on his back, his handful of meal, his bit of salt.

"Gum, Maud,"
most of the boys
were saying, glad
even for that for their
penny. "Juleps," one
said, "red jawbreakers,
some hearts, some
nigger babies—"

He stepped over a low wall but didn't notice where he was
until he saw the large stone bases of pillars all around him.
He stopped. Touched stone. Ran dirt through his fingers.

Always conscious of the Wall, he went slowly from site to
site, from the Praetorium to the Temple of Mithras, as if he
were not aware which way he was tending.

With his handkerchief
still to his nose, he
picked up his coat and
went away.

He stood on the wall.

Tostig was banished
and was killed at
Stamford Bridge
attempting to return
with the aid of
Harold Hardrada,
king of Norway (1066).

The light was already fading but he could see very well.
He blessed the long English twilight. He had a sense of
looking out over vast and dangerous distances. He had a
sense that he had come out very high over everything. And
indeed the Wall was built along the edge of a low escarp-
ment. Broken stone lay tumbled at its foot. For a moment

he had to clutch a bush to keep from falling down among the stones. To pursue, if he could, what new boundary? Pursued as ever by what old enemy?

                                                    "Hogwash," his
                                                    wife said.

He pulled his joy together and set off along a well-worn path on the top of the Wall. As he walked, he spread his arms to measure, to remember. "Four could march abreast," he said. He marched on the Wall until the night was quite black. Then he stopped and looked out into the expanded distance. He drank a bottle of Guinness. A fire burned very far off. He watched it carefully until it faded. He hurled the empty bottle into the darkness and pissed after it. Then he got out his flashlight and picked his way back. It was midnight when he came down off the Wall.

During the fourth and
fifth centuries, troops
were withdrawn from
Britain and the Wall
was abandoned.

He came slowly down the slope, touching stone, feeling earth, and took up his position beside the road. For a long time nothing happened. He ate what was left of his biscuits. He drank his other Guinness. Carefully he brushed the crumbs from his clothing. Carefully policed his area: collected fragments of wrapper and the empty bottle and stowed them in his pack.

Harry Percy was
killed at the Battle
of Shrewsbury, and
Falstaff despoiled
his body (1403).

Then he was aware of cars approaching from opposite directions. The first to reach him was headed in the direction from which he had come. He stood beside the road with his arm outstretched. "Newcastle," he said. The car didn't stop. He ran to the other side of the road and held out his arm. "Carlisle," he said. The car didn't stop.

Byrhtnoth was massacred
by the Danes at Maldon
(991). His followers
died around him:

"A real man knows
where he's going,"
his wife said.

Mind must be firmer   heart must be fiercer
courage must be greater   as our might lessens.

As the tail lights of the cars got farther and farther apart, he felt himself being drawn in a vacuum, expanding and expanding after them.

A View of
the Mountains

It was snowing by the time they got to the Alhambra gardens, but the orange trees were unconcerned. The geraniums might just as well have been in a hothouse. And the fountains went right on, as if it were in the middle of summer, playing forever the Moorish water music. The gardens were deserted, which made them something very special and which, besides, was just as well, because Ben was coming down with something and had to step into shrubbery to be sick.

He knew he ought to go straight to bed, but they had come too far, and there was so little time, and if it had taken him forty years to get to Granada of the Moors, his chances of ever seeing it again were pretty slim. He felt better for a while after he was sick, and they threw snowballs at each other. He thought he was doing it so that he could remember throwing snowballs in Granada. His wife just thought it was mad—at least he guessed that's what she thought. He hoped so anyway, because he wanted her to think of herself as having been mad for once, like someone in a book with a better plot.

By then he was beginning to feel very sick. His legs were weak, and he was almost ready for a day in bed. He hung on, though, for a little longer, and he was glad he did. The snow had stopped. A low gray overcast rushed past in shreds and tatters. He looked out across the valley—not very far, he would have said. Then he noticed patches of white beginning to appear on the overcast. He was about to suggest that white clouds might mean that the weather was changing, that there might be some sun. He was looking at a white cloud when the overcast shifted again, and he fell through—miles and miles through—to a snow-covered mountain. "The Sierra Nevadas," he said aloud, and he shivered, not with cold and not with sickness. It was just the mountain.

He didn't really know that there were in Spain any mountains called the Sierra Nevadas, and if there were any such mountains, he wasn't sure that the mountains he was looking at were the ones. It was just that there always used to be Sierra Nevadas in boys' books, so his vocabulary was up to that small and conscientious demonstration of surprise and delight. He shivered again. "You're sick," his wife said. She was right and he was ready to admit it.

She got him back to the hotel and put him to bed and found a doctor—an English-speaking doctor even. And the doctor didn't say he would come in the evening or in the morning. He simply put on his hat and coat and went along with her, a half-mile or more on foot, talking all the while, far better than a guide. It turned out that there was nothing at all seriously wrong with Ben, just one of those things that happen to travelers. The doctor left a fifty-cent prescription and advised yogurt, four cents a jar. When it came to the bill, Ben and Laura tried to be as delicate as the doctor was, and they finally persuaded him to accept a copy of the Portable Hemingway which was on the bedside table. Ben was sure the doctor would have refused if he had known it was irreplaceable, but it seemed absolutely the right gift for a man who had suddenly made Hemingway seem less of a fraud.

There were some churches they had planned to see in the afternoon. Ben urged his wife to leave him to sleep. "I'll go once you're asleep," she said.

"I'll try to be quick about it."

"That doctor was very nice," she said, "and we'll never see him again."

"Just as well," Ben said. "If we did see him, it would probably be bad for the image."

"Perhaps," she said. She would have argued if he had been well. She was an incurable romantic.

"The mountains were nice, too," she said after a moment. Being in Spain and reading Hemingway had done something to her rhetoric.

"Very nice," he said.

"Would you want to see them again?"

"I've seen them before," he said.

That took a lot of explaining, because she knew perfectly well that he had never before in his life been anywhere near Spain. "It was a long time ago," he said. "I hadn't met you yet. There was never any reason to mention it—there still is really nothing to mention. After all, we don't go around talking haikus to each other: I saw a mountain cloud-strewn in the rain, and my heart laughed with sadness. Under normal circumstances, you must admit, that wouldn't mean much of anything."

"These circumstances seem to be pretty normal," she said. Perhaps she thought his mind was wandering.

"It was at a time when I thought I might be a writer, and I had somehow managed to get myself invited for the summer to an artists' colony in southern Vermont. You know that much at least. I've probably told you about the people who were there that summer. You've even met Bill Watson, come to think of it. He was just as gray and grizzled and beat-up-looking then as he is now. He hadn't published a thing yet, but he was under contract for a novel. The two of us used to go into town every night to drink beer and maybe watch the fights on TV. Sometimes we'd go in Bill's car. Sometimes we'd walk. That was a remarkable thing about Bill. He always left the keys of his car on the mail table and whoever wanted the car first drove it off. The car was just as gray and beat-up-looking as Bill himself, but it ran very well. We all enjoyed it all summer. Personally I thought his gesture with the keys was just a gesture until the first night we wanted to go drink beer and the car was missing. 'I guess we walk tonight,' Bill said, and that was all he said about it—ever."

"You told me he did the same with his Thunderbird after he made some money," she said.

"And so he did. But that was much later. Sometimes we went to town alone. Sometimes there were a few young poets along. Sometimes a painter or two, and sometimes even the great Robert Hatcher, who was in a way giving the place tone that summer."

"You sound bitter," she said.

"No," Ben said, "I didn't mean to. He did look very great to me in those days with his books and his career and all. He was very generous, too, with the younger poets. He would talk prosody with them by the hour, and he would rattle off yards of Yeats with the most infatuated of them. He even read their manuscripts. Perhaps that was why he liked to come with Bill and me sometimes. I mean, we were prose writers, for one thing, and we didn't want anything of him. We were also older and somewhat more buttoned up.

"Anyway, there were some nights—only once in a while—when we all went into town together, and then it was one grand mixture of prosody and beer and Yeats and the fights. That was OK with me. All I didn't want was for someone to start in on Form in the Novel. And I noticed, too, that even the poets must have wanted a rest once in a while, because sooner or later most of them started to hang around the painters' studios, trying their hands at a sketch or two. I wrote a poem myself."

"You never told me," she said.

"It was a haiku," he said.

"One of the things we always talked about at these big sessions was taking Hatcher home in style when he left. He wasn't exactly going home, but he was going to meet his wife in Montpelier and then slip off into some orbit of his own—I think he had a place on the Maine coast. The plan was to fill Bill's car with poets and let Hatcher burst upon Montpelier like a god surrounded by his retinue. Hatcher fell in with the plan and helped embroider it. There were going to be competitions to produce suitable lines to be declaimed on arrival, lines to accompany libations, a small epic to be sung after eating, and an epilogue to be chanted chorally by all the young poets as they receded into the mountains, vine leaves in their hair and all that sort of thing.

"For once Bill Watson stood on the rights of property and insisted on driving the car himself. I don't blame him in the least: writers of fiction have to take scenes where they can get them, and that scene promised to be a particularly good one. But, as it turned out, the poets must have been talking some code among themselves, because when the day at last arrived, there was only Bill standing beside the car with Hatcher. Hatcher himself didn't seem to expect the others, but Bill wanted someone to ride back with him, so he came and pulled me away from my desk. He violated all the rules of the place by breaking in on my working time like that, but it didn't matter in the least. When I got back, the work was waiting on my desk right where I left it.

"There are good roads up either side of the state, but we elected, God knows why, to go up a lesser road through the middle. We stopped awhile at Bread Loaf and looked the people over. Bill and I suggested that Robert Frost lived nearby, and we hoped secretly that Hatcher would take us to see him. Just seeing him would have been enough, but with Hatcher along we might have got handshakes too and a few polite words.

" 'I had forgotten about Frost,' Hatcher said. 'Do you know where he lives?'

"Of course we didn't know. 'Let's try the Post Office,' Bill said.

"That was good sound technique but it didn't work. Everybody was sworn to protect Robert Frost from strangers, which was fair enough. 'Perhaps they'll tell you,' Bill said.

" 'I don't like to presume,' Hatcher said.

" 'There must be some kind of office for the conference where we can ask,' I said. I really wanted to see Robert Frost.

" 'There's sure to be somebody I'd have to visit with,' Hatcher said. 'We'd never get home.'

"I was myself perfectly willing to visit endlessly with people Hatcher knew. Before that summer I had never met a single person who wrote anything at all. It was all very new to me, and I was game for any writer I had ever heard of. We both deferred to Hatcher, however, and got into the car and headed north once more."

"Where were the mountains all this time?" his wife asked.

"They were all around us," Ben said. "Our way lay along a valley between two ranges of mountains, except we couldn't see them very well. Rain fell all day, sometimes in blinding showers. Sometimes clouds hid the mountains completely. Sometimes we even drove through clouds. Vistas opened suddenly in the rain. One moment there was nothing to see and then there was a quick glimpse of rocks, trees, vast shapes, more like a dream than any landscape. I think perhaps no one has ever seen that country but the three of us in the car that day. And I know I have never seen anything like it until today. Even changing a tire in the rain couldn't spoil the picture.

"In the end, of course, we came to Montpelier. I was hungry and happy and looked forward to cleaning up and having a drink and a good meal. We drove into the yard and got out and began to unload Hatcher's gear. Hatcher, who was last in the car, reached over and honked the horn. At once from deep within the house there came a lovely feminine scream, high, clear, and entirely suited to the supposed occasion, the occasion that had so often been discussed among beer and prosody and Yeats and the fights. The voice itself was as fine as the whole ride through the rain. 'Where are the young poets?' were the actual words, but I heard a lot more—*Io, Apollo,* for instance, and things even more foolish than that, *Bacchus,* perhaps, and *Venus.* Then, standing in the rain, tugging at a suitcase in the trunk of Bill's old car, I saw Bill, dirty, grizzled, and I saw myself.

"Needless to say, the women who were there had impeccable manners. They gave us a lot to drink and a lot to eat, and they laughed at whatever we found to say, and they never once reminded us that we weren't after all poets or young or anything of the sort. It was very nice, I'm sure, but my memory stops with the scream and the rest is really a blank."

"You weren't that old even when I met you," she said.

"You have the best manners in the world," Ben said. "Now I want to sleep."

He did sleep, too, and she went out to see a church he would never see. Her manners were so good, in fact, that she didn't pretend the church was overrated and described it to him in great detail next day on the train when it was raining so hard there was absolutely nothing to see.

Perhaps Love

Paul and Emily were in love. At least Paul thought they were. There was no way he could tell what Emily thought. She never talked about it. "Hush," she would say if he tried to work around to the subject. He listened to what she said and to what she didn't say, and he tried reading her eyes and the condition of her skin and the texture of her hair. He deduced that she was healthy and sleeping well, and if she had been a horse or a dog he would have bought her on the spot, but he still didn't know if she loved him.

When he came right down to it, he wasn't sure that he loved her. Really sure, that is. He often discussed it with her—inside his head, of course.

Paul: The stop light of that car ahead of us—

Emily: Yes, it's red.

Paul: That's just the point. We agree that it's red.

Emily: We agree completely.

Paul: But the real point is that we have both learned to call that red.

Emily: It is red.

Paul: Of course it's red. But how can I ever be sure that what I am seeing is the same thing you are seeing?

Emily: I see red.

Paul: And I see red.

Emily: We see the same thing.

Paul: Right.

Emily: So we both see red.

Paul: But how do I know that the image on my retina is the same as the image on your retina?

Emily: You don't.

Paul: Well, then, my retina might be showing what your retina would call green.

Emily: That's pretty silly, you know.

Paul: I know.

And Paul found it the same with love. He thought he was in love with Emily, but never having known what it was that other people felt and called love, he wasn't sure. He read books about sex and novels about love, but the conventional symptoms didn't seem to fit his case. He slept well. He could concentrate on his work. He didn't seem to be losing his mind. He was, however, losing weight, but he felt well and alert and was quite confident he was in all respects exactly as usual—except, of course, for being in love—perhaps. But his friends noticed something.

Friend: You're looking a bit thinner, Paul.

Paul: I have lost a little weight.

Friend: Perhaps you're not sleeping right?

Paul: Never slept better in my life.

Friend: Perhaps you've got something on your mind?

Paul: I've a mind like a newborn babe.

Friend: Perhaps it's that Emily? Fucking yourself to death, man?

Paul: Not exactly.

Friend: Go on.

Paul: Really.

The truth is that Paul's wife took a dim view of anyone else fucking Paul to death, and although Emily's husband didn't much care, he didn't really think it should be Emily, and both batches of children were steadfastly against the whole thing. Not that this made the least difference to Paul and Emily. They went on doing their thing even if the thing wasn't exactly what Paul had imagined when he used to think about such things as An Affair and The Other Woman. Like his friends, he had imagined that one simply fucked himself to death. What a way to go, he had imagined. It hadn't occurred to him that a love affair might involve as much as walking through fields and watching the wind ripple on grass and watching the sun glitter on water, the rain dapple pavements, as did a foreign art film, as many headaches, periods, and fatigues as did a marriage. Nor had it occurred to him that a love affair might make him happy. He had never imagined past the fucking. Well, happiness, like love, like red lights—who knows? At least he wasn't still miserable.

He had been very miserable. Of course his wife had been miserable, too.

Wife: But it's togetherness.

Paul: It's what we have.

Wife: And if we have togetherness at all, why can't we have good togetherness?

Paul: I want you to write on my tombstone: He et what was set before him.

Wife: Is that a crack about my cooking?

Paul: It wasn't supposed to be.

Wife: But I can take it that way if I want? You bastard.

Paul: I wasn't even thinking about your cooking.

Wife: It's so bad you can't bear to think about it, is it?

Paul: I was just trying to fall in with your mood.

Wife: You really need to hate me, don't you? You have to believe I'm a lousy cook so you can justify yourself in your own eyes for wanting a younger woman.

Paul: A younger woman?

Wife: Do you think I'm blind?

And Emily had been very miserable. And, of course, her husband had been miserable, too.

Husband: I won't be home for supper tonight.

Emily: I was planning—

Husband: Sorry, these clients from out of town—

Emily: Will you be late?

Husband: Don't wait up.

Emily: The lamb will keep another day.

Husband: With garlic? My favorite.

Emily: I know.

Husband: But tomorrow is my bowling night, and I'll have to go straight from work.

Emily: What a bore.

Husband: Isn't it?

Emily: One day soon?

Husband: Of course.

Paul's wife was right about one thing—Emily was a younger woman. She was a lot younger. Paul wasn't sure that was why he wanted her, but there was no getting around the fact that she was younger. A different generation entirely. He thought of old—older, that is—of older men who had married young women. He thought of Charlie Chaplin. When Chaplin married Oona O'Neill, Paul had thought it was just another of his comedies, probably a comedy in poor taste. But as the years passed (and Chaplin never seemed to get any older), Paul, despairing of love, began to look on it as a tragedy. He suspected that Chaplin had probably slipped over into the role of Emil Jannings in *The Blue Angel.* Then he met Emily and discovered that an older man could actually fall in love. But still there was the doubt.

Emily's Little Boy: I'm cold.

Paul: Sit on the bench now and wrap up in the towel while I change out of my bathing suit.

Boy: Why are your feet so small? Their feet are big.

Paul: Some people have big feet, and some people have little feet.

Boy: Why is your weenie all wrinkled up?

Paul: I guess I'm cold, too.

Boy: When are you going to die?

Paul: No one can tell when he's going to die. But if you find out, let me know, will you?

Boy: You're going to die tomorrow.

Paul lived the next twenty-four hours warily. It had never really been brought home to him how many deaths brushed past him in a normal day. He crossed streets only on walk lights. He stayed out of the pool. He played with his food until his wife had tasted hers. When he saw Emily's little girl's blocks on the stairs, he knew why they were there. He even made an excuse not to go to bed with Emily, a rare and fleeting chance, because of a possible heart attack. And he

knew he had the heart of a man twenty years younger. He finally re-
signed himself to sleeping in his own bed only after making sure that
his wife was asleep and that all the kitchen knives were in their
place. And the day passed.

Paul: I had a dream.

Emily: I love dreams.

Paul: Are dreams allowed?

Emily: They're lovely.

Paul: I dreamed of a dinner.

Emily: Are you sure you're eating right?

Paul: I think I forget to eat sometimes.

Emily: Very bad.

Paul: I'll try to do better.

Emily: I'll have to take you in hand. Are you feeling all right?

Paul: I feel fine. Really fine.

Emily: We have to keep your strength up.

Paul: I think it was good for me to lose some weight.

Emily: But how about the dinner?

Paul: What dinner?

Emily: The dinner in your dream.

Paul: It was very strange. There I was at the table. You were
running back and forth to the kitchen.

Emily: Very likely.

Paul: I said, For god's sake, sit down, Molly. That's an old family
joke.

Emily: You've told me.

Paul: Sorry, I forget a lot.

Emily: Don't be sorry.

Paul: Opposite me were a man and a woman. They weren't at all
clear but they were dressed conservatively. The man was
wearing a coat and vest. I think they were older. They could
have been your parents—or mine—or me in relation to you, you
know.

Emily: We don't talk about that.

Paul: I seem to dream about it.

Emily: Not allowed.

Paul: And lounging against the wall was this youth. God, just standing there he was insufferable. And the people opposite—I think of them as Witnesses—said, "And what will you call yourselves when you are married?"

Emily: Censored.

Paul: It's in the dream.

Emily: Try to dream more carefully.

Paul: I didn't know what to say—in the dream, I mean—but the Youth said, "Oh, we'll call ourselves Paul or Paul and Emily or Emily-Paul." While he was saying this, you were bending over and kissing my head and neck and rubbing your head against mine to show them it was really me, but they didn't pay any attention, neither the Witnesses nor the Youth.

Emily: Then what?

Paul: Then I woke up. It had turned cold in the night, and I had a terrible cramp in my foot.

Emily: So what do you make of it?

Paul: Even while I was walking up and down to ease my foot, it was no problem for me to know that Youth. It was me as I ought to be for you.

Emily: That's your opinion.

The rain was dappling the pavement. The wind was rippling on the grass. Cloud shadows counterpointed the wind over the subtle swells of the prairie. Paul's office building was a very high place, standing up out of the flat land like a tower of Pisa built by incompetent engineers. The sun glittered on distant stock ponds. Paul knew enough now not to talk about it, and he almost believed Emily saw what he saw—but not quite. He was waiting for that to come.

Paul: I used to think it would be like *Brief Encounter.*

Emily: What on earth do you mean?

Paul: I mean—let me see—well, something like—a man my age—

Emily: What age?

Paul: A man falling in love and finding that it was somehow too late, that circumstances had him irrevocably trapped, so he could only view, briefly, a happiness that might have been.

Emily: Those people had too much character.

Paul: It's character that made the Empire great.

Emily: And I used to think it would be like *Madame Bovary*.

Paul: I'm with you there—or I was once. Once upon a time. I did a project on *Madame Bovary* in college. The professor hated to read so I did drawings and mock-ups. Anything went in that class—except writing. One girl acted the part of Emma. She took an underdose of poison and said she did it out of love for the professor. She got an A. One guy acted the part of Rodolphe and had an affair with the professor's wife. He got knocked down by the professor's car, but he lived and got his A.

Emily: That was some school you went to.

Paul: It was the hissing of Emma's corset strings that got me. You know, when she was in such a hurry to get to bed. Just thinking about it still almost smothers me.

Emily: Shall I wear a corset for you?

Paul: You're laughing at me.

Emily: I'm not laughing.

Paul: Sssssssssss.

Emily: I'm not crying either.

Paul: What was it with you about the book? The cab bucketing from one end of the city to the other all those hours?

Emily: I think it was her dreams, what she wanted. It was very sad.

Paul knew better than to mention a rainbow. There it was. She couldn't miss it. He wasn't quite sure what he could say. He was smothering but he felt he would have to say something. His secretary would be back at any moment. He glanced down at the street. There she was, crossing from the Court House to the Coffee Shoppe. In ten minutes she would come out, chewing a toothpick, which she would deposit in the sand pot at the elevator. She had been with him a very long time, and each knew pretty well what the other would stand. Actually it was a double rainbow, although you had to look very carefully for the second one.

Paul: There's something on my mind.

Emily: Then you better get it off.

Paul: It was that time, you know, that time last week, when I couldn't go to bed with you.

Emily: What about it?

Paul: I can't quite sort it all out in my head. I mean, it seemed all right at the time, but since then I can't stop thinking about it.

Emily: You think too much.

Paul: As you have often remarked.

Emily: As I have often remarked.

Paul: But what I think about is what you think.

Emily: I won't say I never think, but I certainly didn't think about that.

Paul: I think maybe you think I wasn't eager enough.

Emily: Nonsense.

Paul: I think maybe you think I'm not man enough.

Emily: I'll give you a certificate in writing if you want.

Paul: You're sure you didn't think?

Emily: Hush.

Paul: I feel better now.

Emily: Here comes the dragon to your door.

Paul: There she is. You're sitting on the strap of my binoculars. Thank you. Yes, chewing her toothpick.

Emily: So I'll pick you up here at 1:00 on Saturday.

Paul: Right.

Emily: You're sure you don't mind the kids?

Paul: I've seen kids before.

Emily: Right.

Paul had indeed seen kids before. He had seen plenty of them, but it had been a long time since he had seen them so young. Still, it was a good age. He remembered it with pleasure. Not that his own kids weren't OK now. He liked them. None of them had gone out of his way to make him a grandfather. They were expensive to keep up but they were OK. Burned a lot of oil and the mileage wasn't so good. Dependable though. Very dependable.

It was the camping, actually, that bothered him more than the kids. It was the sheer lunacy of giving up comfort and convenience in favor of doing everything the hardest possible way. Living naturally, indeed. What was natural for a civilized human being was meals at the table at regular hours, sleep in a good and familiar bed, the repose of not having to break your ass to get somewhere to seek repose. Of course he might like it. He knew himself enough to guess that much of his distaste for camping came from never having camped. Here was an unknown situation in which he might prove a fool. Well, it had to be risked.

Emily: I'm taking the kids camping this weekend.

Husband: Mmmm. What?

Emily: I'm taking the kids camping this weekend.

Husband: Good.

Emily: We're going way up into the lakes.

Husband: That's nice.

Emily: It will be something for them while you're at your conference.

Husband: Mmmm.

and

Paul: My sick friend, Bunbury—

Wife: You bastard.

They went way up into the lakes. With careful planning, with discreet pretexts offered, they set off on what Paul couldn't help viewing as his Tenderfoot Test. It wasn't exactly what he had imagined when he tried to contrive a weekend with Emily, but it was better than nothing. Much better, although he was at a complete loss as to where the fucking came in. With the kids in the tent and all. Still, they would be together. Fucking wasn't really what it was all about exactly.

The rain was pocking the mud. The wind blew the rain in white gusts through the headlights. The windshield wipers couldn't suck up all the water, but Emily still pulled the car carefully off the edge of the forest track and eased into a small clearing. Paul wasn't sure if he was more afraid of going on or stopping.

Emily: This is a campsite.

Paul: If you say so.

Emily: Here's the plan.

Paul: You're in charge.

Emily: We bed the kids down for the night on the seats of the car.
Paul: Ah.
Emily: It's so late now and so wet and that will be best.
Paul: Right.
Emily: Then we take the tent out of the trunk, spread it out in the headlights, put the frame together, peg the tent, and so to bed.
Paul: Right.
Emily: Poor dear, you haven't a clue, have you?
Paul: Right.
Emily: It's a jointed aluminum external frame, but you'll see.
Paul: Let's go.
Emily: It shouldn't take more than ten minutes.

Paul: There's a piece missing.
Emily: What?
Paul: One of the curved pieces is missing, so the support just shoots off at an angle and doesn't go down to the ground.
Emily: Damn.
Paul: I suppose I could stand and hold it.
Emily: You won't do that, nor will I, no.
Paul: Wait. I'll let the car roll up to the tent and rest the support on the hood.
Emily: My husband will kill me if it scratches his hood.
Paul: I'll rest it in my sneaker.
Emily: Good thinking.
Paul: No sooner said than done.
Emily: Now we're back on the beam. What we do now is get the sleeping bags out of the trunk and zip them together.
Paul: Ah.
Emily: Then we go up to the shelter and take a good hot shower and leave our clothes in the drying room and wear our raincoats back here.
Paul: Right.

Emily: Are you warm enough?
Paul: Lovely.

Emily: Lovely body warmth. You'll be a lovely camper.
Paul: Emily—
Emily: Hush.
Paul: Hush it is.
The rain drummed on the canvas. The wind flapped the canvas.
And they fell instantly into a very deep, very satisfying sleep.

The Eclipse

It was an awful day in a series of awful days. All morning—it was the fifth Wednesday morning in a row—Mason had sat in the courthouse lobby across from his wife, pretending to read in order to avoid meeting her eyes or seeming to listen when she talked with her lawyer. He tried to listen of course, but he could hear very little. He wondered what her lawyer was saying to her. When his own lawyer came out and talked to him, he still wondered what was being said. And when the two lawyers went back into the judge's chambers arm in arm, he wondered what they said to each other, what to the judge. He felt at times as if he were standing at a supermarket checkout, watching aghast as the clerk rang up an endless tape of items he hadn't intended to buy. Often they were alone in the lobby with the statue of Lincoln, a hand extended to each of them but eyes still fiercely on Stephen Douglas. She knitted row after row, upstaging him as usual. He could only bring a book, a solid respectable book, and make sure he had it right side up and kept his head bent over it.

His lawyer came out at noon and said, "That's all for today." Mason shrugged. He was no longer outraged.

The lawyer assumed a stance like Lincoln and said—probably with an eye on his biographer—"'The hungry judges soon the sentence sign,/ And wretches hang that jury-men may dine.'" He was a very literary sort of lawyer.

"Just so," Mason said. He started for the stairs.

"Next Wednesday," the lawyer called after him.

"Same time, same place," Mason said without turning.

"Just so," the lawyer said. It was his phrase after all.

Mason turned his back on his office and instinctively walked in the direction where he would meet open country the soonest. He chose back streets, mostly deserted, for he felt himself surrounded by a force field of gloom and despair, an object of loathing to himself and others. He knew they could feel what he was, and he didn't want to see it in their faces. That would be too much. Especially he didn't want to see it in Sandy's face.

"You aren't really like that, Mr. Mason," she had said. She was a kid then, a student at the university working part-time in his office.

"Like what?"

"Like the things you say."

"Such as what?"

"Such as, 'Most men live lives of quiet desperation.' "

"Don't they?"

"I don't believe it, and I don't think you do either."

"I think I do."

"You're putting yourself on," she said.

"Good lord," he said. "What a language."

"And you don't believe men's lives are 'nasty, brutish, and short' either."

"But if I think I believe it, how can you say I don't?"

"I just feel it."

"That's getting pretty esoteric for me," he said.

"It's just something I sense. I don't listen to you really."

"Well, thank you very much."

"You know what I mean, Mr. Mason."

"Of course I do, but it's all very tenuous." His vocabulary was very refined in those days.

"It's what I feel," she said. "I feel it very strongly." She walked out of the office one day and walked in again ten years later. Mason had thought about her from time to time, and after five years or so of thinking decided he should have fucked her. It would have been statutory rape then, and his wife might have had him thrown in jail. But then, she might have divorced him. Who knows?

"Hello, Mr. Mason," she said when she came back.

"Long coffee break," Mason said.

"I was trying for the record," she said.

"My wife set that," Mason said. "She went out in aught and fifty and isn't back yet. Still on the payroll. Twenty-two years. You're just a piker but I'm glad to see you."

"I'm glad to see you, too," Mr. Mason," she said.

"Perhaps we can drop that Mr. Mason stuff," Mason said.

"OK."

"Unless you're coming back to work, of course."

"No, I don't think so."

"Too bad."

"You might say we have some unfinished business, though," she said.

"You might say that," Mason said. So they finished—or began—it that afternoon. He had had a lot of time to think about it.

And that was what at last had brought him into court after twenty years—more—of marriage. He thought he had discovered what it was all about. He went around smiling at people. People even smiled at him. He thought he had discovered what he was really like. He wasn't Old Gruff-and-Grim after all. Not that he was exactly an enchanted prince, although he felt pretty fine most of the time. A weight that had been on his shoulders fell off—a house, a wife, children, a business, all fell off and rolled away somewhere out of sight. He straightened up and looked around him. He walked on the balls of his feet. A new man—a rediscovered man. At once he wanted to make an honest woman of Sandy, but she didn't see it that way at all.

"Marry?" she said. "After ten rotten years of rotten marriage? I'd have to be crazy."

"Oh," Mason said. He hadn't thought about it that way. He guessed he was an incurable romantic.

"I'm the incurable romantic," she said. "I keep thinking there's got to be something better than marriage."

The question proved to be academic in any case, because his wife laughed at the idea of divorce. "Keep your whore," she said. "I'm keeping the house and the car and the paycheck and the insurance and the retirement and the social security and Medicare and Medicaid and the eleventh *Britannica*."

"What do I get?" Mason said foolishly.

"Fair is fair," she said. "You get what you want, and I get what I want."

So there they sat week after week in court while the lawyers got what they wanted.

The street he was walking along was very quiet. It wasn't a through street. There were stop signs at every corner. The trees were large and old. In places the brick sidewalks were completely overgrown by grass. The small clapboard houses were close to the sidewalk but very private, with large vine-covered porches.

At first Mason had to go on living at home. His wife kept all the money, and he couldn't afford to live anywhere else. Sometimes Sandy took him out to dinner when her alimony check came in, but mostly he ate at home, which wasn't as bad as it might have been, because his wife rarely spoke to him and wouldn't eat with him. At least he didn't have to listen to her jaw click as she chewed. It wasn't perfect but it was still a lot better than before Sandy.

He was better. Even when fits of his old despair returned, he knew he was better. He laughed sometimes—he laughed a lot. It was like old times with his own family when he was little. There had been laughter then. Sandy had changed him completely. He positively radiated, and he could prove it by the girl with the flowers.

That was a rainy afternoon in winter. He was walking home through the park from Sandy's. He was just going to go in and eat whatever his wife set before him and hang on to that island of joy square in the middle of himself. He was walking along in the rain, hanging on, wearing his old army poncho with his head as hidden as a monk's. Vaguely he was aware of someone overtaking him, but he didn't pay any attention until he heard a woman say, "Hold out your hands." Without thinking, he disengaged his hands from his poncho and held them out. Like magic they cradled a bowl of flowers. "I could tell you would like them," she said and went on. "Thank you," he whispered. It *was* like magic. She had had only a shapeless mass to go on as she overtook him. It had to be pure feeling. A month ago she would have run past screaming.

His wife didn't think much of the flowers. "Flower Arranging I at the university," she said. "Any fool can see that. She probably had a roomful already."

"Perhaps," he said, but he couldn't believe less in the magic.

"Or did your whore give them to you to butter me up with? Ugly arrangement."

"Perhaps," he said.

"Or has your whore run off with a younger stud at last, so you bought them for me yourself? How touching."

"Perhaps," he said. He was hanging on for dear life, but he was hanging on.

He saw that he was about to pass an old VW bus parked at the curb. He recognized it now. He had walked here at night. There were two hounds that lived in the bus and sprang out as he passed. They scared him stiff. Now, he rather wished they would spring out. He'd like to see how they reacted. He must be giving off a really lovely stink—terror added to despair—but it was always possible that the dogs would sense something else, something even he couldn't be sure of. But the bus was empty, although the stench of the dogs sickened him as he passed. Maybe they only work at night, he thought, but he wasn't sure if he was relieved or disappointed.

"It's crazy," he said to Sandy. "This whole business is crazy. I can't sit down in the middle of a field without having a kitten in my lap within seconds. I'll bet if I tried to cross Times Square at 3 A.M. some nice old lady would grab my arm and see me across."

"That's a crock of shit," Sandy said.

"What's a crock of shit?" Mason said. Knowing her had done something to his vocabulary.

"That feeling business is a crock of shit."

"I learned it from you," he said.

"The body replaces each and every cell within seven years," she said. "I am not the person you learned it from."

"Oh," he said, "I thought it was you."

"You have a lot to learn," she said. She was right, of course. He could only be humble.

He had his own opinion, however. And things were improving. Not fast enough to suit him but definitely improving. Especially since the judge had allowed him to keep a little of his check, enough for a cheap apartment and a pound of hamburger now and then. He had thought it might be easier if he and Sandy pooled their hamburger, shared an apartment, but she wasn't ready to live with anyone. In a way he was grateful. He was grateful at night when he was too tired to be polite to anyone and when he needed the whole bed to toss in. He was grateful when he was too awful in the morning. And he was grateful when he just wanted to scratch himself and fart and go to sleep. He wanted to live with Sandy and would have sacrificed these luxuries for her, but he knew they were luxuries and enjoyed them. They were doing him good. Everything was doing him good.

Take the spacey old man in the supermarket. Space calling to space. Mason had been working all night—spending afternoons with Sandy had put him behind in his work. He thought he would just buy himself a little liver for breakfast—another luxury of living alone. His wife never gave him liver because she didn't like the smell. Everything was very clear and deep in the early morning light. He felt he was walking just a little off the floor, perhaps enough to slide a sheet of paper under the soles of his boots. He didn't think anyone would notice, but as he was struggling to free a grocery cart from the stack, an old man came up and said, "Howdy."

"Oh," Mason said, freeing his cart at last, "lovely morning, isn't it?"

The old man took a cart and came along. "A little cold," he said.

Mason was uneasy with people who said Howdy. Either they had you sized up or they were hiding behind it like a beard. The old man had a beard too, but he looked very much the real thing. "Seasonal," Mason said.

"Time to buy seed for my birds," the old man said. "They'll be back any day now."

"Yes indeed," Mason said, moving on.

"I must feed a hundred during the winter," the old man said, keeping pace. "They'll be back soon. The teal have gone. I saw two flights. They're the first."

"Early for geese," Mason said. He wondered how the old man knew that the one nice thing he took when he moved out of the house was his binoculars, his good bird glasses and the hand-made case he had designed himself.

"The geese hang on until the last minute," the old man said. He stopped beside the sacks of birdseed.

"Sometimes even after," Mason said. He stopped too. "I've seen some waxwings."

"What do you know?" the old man said. "I guess I missed them this year. Glad to hear of them, though."

"Have a good winter," Mason said. He went off toward the meats.

"Same to you," the old man called. "Lots of birds."

Mason waited at a corner for a car to pass, but it sat at the stop sign until he reluctantly looked at the driver and was waved ahead. Coincidence, he said to himself. Just a lonely old man wanting someone to talk to. There was no help there. It had been an awful day. He was awful.

"Would you like to see the eclipse?" someone said. Mason kept going. But he glanced at the sky involuntarily. The sky had cleared. There was going to be an eclipse, almost a total eclipse. It would be visible after all. There had been something about it in the paper, but he had paid little attention. Perhaps it was taking place right now. He knew better than to look at the sun, though.

"Take the glass," his mother said, "and hold it carefully by the edges. Don't rub the smoke off, or the sun will hurt your eyes." They were standing in the driveway between the two houses to keep out of the wind. The sun looked very strange through the dark glass. It was a dark disk with a bright crown. "This is very educational," his mother said. She put her arm around him and drew him tight against the cold fur of her coat. It was soft and smelled lovely like her closet.

"I say, would you like to see the eclipse?" the voice said again. Although it couldn't be speaking to him, Mason stopped. There was no one else who could be spoken to. There was no one who could be speaking. He looked all around carefully and was about to go on when he caught a slight movement among the vine leaves on the nearest porch. Then he saw an old man's face peering out at him. My god, he thought, am I getting to be a crazy old man myself? Can they smell me?

"Would you?" the old man said. He skipped down the steps.

"Why yes," Mason said. "I would. Yes," he said, "I really would."

"I've made a device," the old man said. "I saw how to do it in the paper." He was a thin, straight old man, very shabby. Mason guessed a professor retired so long ago that his pension had become almost worthless. "Look," he said. He held up a cardboard box, long and narrow. It was rather like a periscope.

"Yes," Mason said. He handled it gently. He was impressed. He knew he could never make a periscope from directions in the paper. Sometimes he was discouraged by things like that, but now the old man's pleasure outweighed everything.

"Point the top at the sun and look down at the bottom." Mason studied the white paper at the bottom of the box, straining for something too faint for him to see. The old man placed both delicate hands on the device and moved it slightly.   "Yes," Mason said. "Yes, there it is." And there it was, a small but perfect image of the sun with a small but perfect bite out of the side.

"It's wonderful," Mason said.

"Isn't it?" the old man said.

"I don't know how to thank you," Mason said. "I had forgotten all about it and would have missed it completely." He handed the periscope back to the old man, who received it lightly on his out-stretched palms. "I must be getting on," he said. It was nearly time to call Sandy to report that nothing had happened again. It was only what they expected, but he had to hear her say it didn't matter.

The old man took another look at the sun. Mason looked, too. They said goodbye.

As he went back through the dappled shade, he thought, It *is* all right. It's not awful at all.

Power Line

The power line wasn't showing up where Mason expected it to be. To be sure, the path kept bearing around to the north, but even so he ought to have hit the power line long before this—at least if it was anywhere near where he spotted it from the bus yesterday. If it didn't show up soon, he would have to turn back to the highway and pick it up farther down, where he had actually seen it. After all, the road might have taken a turn he didn't remember or the power line itself might have angled off in a new direction over behind the hill he had seen it climbing.

A half-hour ago he had thought he saw the glint of insulators through the trees, but the path had veered around a deep ravine—still off there to his left—that surely had water at the bottom, perhaps a great deal of water. Now he had lost all sense of the power line and the path as sides of an angle, and he knew he should stop and go back. Five minutes more, he told himself. Then two. Then just as far as the oak tree at the turn in the path.

At the oak tree he stopped. Stopping was always the hardest part. Giving up all he had committed. But the path was now tending even farther to the north. The sun, which had been behind him to begin with, was now at his right shoulder, and he was going off in exactly the wrong direction—he had planned to hit the power line and turn south.

The only good thing about what had happened was that it justified his decision not to trust to his own guidance in the woods

but to follow the power line, which had, after all, to be going somewhere. He could get himself way out in the woods miles away from
anyone and still not get himself hopelessly lost. Perhaps it was no
worse than using a compass.

He sat with his back against the oak tree and opened his pack.
An apple and a bit of cheese. A can of beer—*vin du pays*. He
would have liked a book but had been unable to decide on the
appropriate one so left it to chance—something found on the bus
or in a country drugstore. So far nothing had turned up. Ideally it
should have been a slim volume in Greek but he didn't read
Greek—couldn't even keep the fraternities straight. Sophocles,
perhaps. Or Pindar. Pindar was always showing up in walkers'
packs: a shirt, a change of socks, cheese, apples, wine, and Pindar,
who the hell ever he was.

Sophocles, of course, showed up in all kinds of drama courses.
You couldn't very well not know Sophocles. And once Mason had
even tried to learn the Greek alphabet. It hadn't taken, though.
Now when he tried to remember it, he only got something from a
football skit they used to do in junior high: alpha, beta, kappa,
gamma, two pi r square, shift.

He woke up one morning after an awful undergraduate drunk to
find his dictionary open on his desk. He looked at it and said
"Alpha" without caring to ask himself why. He walked around it
for a long time before he could engage himself with the matter.
"Beta," he said. He had known that much ever since Picturesque
Word Origins in the Sunday *American:* Alphabet, the first two letters of the Greek alphabet, alpha and beta; Curfew, *couvre feu,*
cover fire; Pumpernickel, dark Russian bread *bon pour nicol* (good
enough for Nicholas, which happened to be the name of the French
trooper's horse); Panic, the sudden appearance of the god Pan,
causing alarm and confusion.

He had danced with her the night before. He disguised himself in
his roommate's tuxedo and went very late to a dance. He was so
drunk by then that he had forgotten he couldn't dance. And he cut
in on her repeatedly—mooned over for months and never spoken
to. And he made a date. For what? For when? He would have to

call her and try to find out—very deviously, of course. And then what? What would a sorority girl expect in the way of a date? It filtered through to him that she had been wearing a Star of David medallion between her breasts. Not exactly the kind of thing he could ask about. Aleph, beth, gimel.

Her name was Eliza Beth Rudolph, but when he got to the dormitory—some sorority girls lived in dormitories—when he got to the dormitory—Eliza Beth Rudolph had never heard of him. She certainly hadn't danced with him and wasn't even at the dance. And yet it was she he had studied in the library and followed on the Broad Walk. He had even changed his schedule to get into a class which she dropped at once. She couldn't help him at all.

"A girl about so tall," he said in sorority after sorority, striking the bridge of his nose with the edge of his hand and indicating someone about five foot ten. Eliza Beth was, in fact, about that height with heels. "With or without heels?" the sorority girls said. "I don't know," he said. As for himself, his roommate's dancing shoes had hurt his feet, so he kicked them off and danced in his stockinged feet most of the night. "Blond or brunette?" they said. "Sort of," he said. Since they didn't ask about the medallion or the mole on her left breast, none of them could help him.

As the week drew to a close—he hoped he had made the date for the weekend—he had finished both sides of Sorority Row and begun on the overflow around the corner, newer, bigger, but less prestigious houses. He smote himself on the nose and she appeared like a nosebleed. And

    she was engaged

    she had no intention of going out with him

    she had been humoring a drunk:

    goodbye

He did not retrace his steps from sorority to sorority, talking again with all the five-foot-ten girls who had been trotted out for him and who thought his story was cute. But, since he thought he had made a date with Eliza Beth, he went back to the dormitory and talked with her again.

"It was your sister," he said.

"I thought it was," she said.

"Then why didn't you tell me?"

"I hoped it would be somebody else. For your sake I hoped it would be somebody else."

"Yes," he said. "Because she's engaged."

"Because she's a shit. Because Rae Beth is a complete shit."

"She's your sister," he said, in his amazement stressing all the words so that he could only hope he had stressed none.

"She stole my boyfriend, and the only thing I can say is that he deserves her."

"I think I thank you," he said.

"Don't thank me," she said. "Thank heaven."

He did, but it was a long time before he thanked heaven again. Eliza Beth's boyfriend was absolutely right. He had started out with the wrong sister and got out fast, leaving a booby trap for the next man to walk into. That was the beginning of Mason's thirty-year mistake.

He crushed the beer can with his hands and stood up. Balancing against the oak tree, he stomped the can with his foot and put it in his pack. Then he started back the way he had come.

It was a long way back, undoing all he had done, whole sections of trail never seen before rising unexpectedly before him. But at last he stood in the meadow where he had hesitated before striking into the woods. A primitive road had brought him this far. He had been expecting a logging site if anything but had found the meadow, warm and still in the autumn sun, and the boarded-up cabin with lawn furniture piled on the screened porch: Regularly Inspected by State Police. Trespassers Will Be Prosecuted.

Again he hesitated at the edge of the meadow. Directly across from him the road took up. In half an hour he could be back on the highway, ready to start again from the beginning—or, no, that wasn't quite true. He had already had a long walk in the woods, and that was what he had come for after all. It wasn't as if there were a plan or a schedule.

He now remembered that on the side of the meadow where he stood there was possibly a second path. He had noticed it as he came along the first time—a slight thinning in the underbrush that might develop into a path on closer inspection. Well, why not? The power line was only a ploy after all. It was time in the woods he really wanted.

Not only was there a path there, but it bore off slightly to the south and seemed likely to skirt the head of the ravine that had forced the other path to the north. So interested was he in checking out this speculation that he was actually standing in the power line right-of-way before he remembered what he had been looking for. He had picked his way through a tangle of downed trees, inexplicably cut and left lying—he checked the stumps to make sure it wasn't storm damage. His eyes were so intent on places to set his feet that he was actually standing hip-deep in ferns before he realized he had come out of the woods. Apparently the power company had been cutting back the edges of its right-of-way.

He stood among the ferns and looked along the line both in the direction he would go and in the direction he would not go. Both ways the vista ended in a hill, and over each hill hawks soared. They were too high and too far away for him to bother with his glasses, but, reminded now, he took the glasses from their case and hung them around his neck. He found, as he expected, a footpath running along near the base of the pylons.

By the time he was halfway up the hill, the hawks had moved on. Something in the back of his head was going thud thud thud. He sat on a boulder beside the path and looked across to the other hill. There were more hawks than ever. Near at hand two flickers scrabbled at the trunk of a dead tree. One flew down to rest on what seemed to be a rick of freshly cut firewood. He strolled over to investigate, walking along a contour to make it easy on himself.

After a few yards of forcing his way through ferns and the tops of downed trees, he struck a beaten path that led him directly to the pile. It was indeed a rick of freshly cut fireplace lengths, much of it split into manageable chunks. Very curious, way out here so far from roads and houses. He began following a maze of paths all around the rick, looking for a path leading in, for a road to truck out the wood. However, the maze seemed perfectly self-contained.

As he studied it more carefully, he saw piles of brush cut off the trunks that had been sawed up. He saw streaks of sawdust on the ground—a foot and a half apart? two feet?—where the logs had been cut. He was pleased with himself for noticing that the streaks were made up of fine sawdust laid down in short patches. It was a two-man saw, he decided. Very different from the mounds of coarse sawdust where the power company's chain saw had felled the trees. Then he checked the ground for footprints and found where the sawyers had stood. A pair of whacking great boots with Vibram soles run over slightly at the heels. He made a print of his own beside a particularly clear one. The other was far larger than his 9, probably a 12, but run over in the same pattern. On the other side of the log, much smaller prints, also Vibram but new. A boy? Father and son in the woods together. Or a woman? The print was very narrow. He printed his own left print beside the small narrow print. It wasn't like a boy's print at all. He put his foot back in his own print and assumed the position of sawing. Ah, he said. She was left-handed. He was always aware of left-handedness because he was himself left-handed. He already liked her. Then he turned around and faced the other way and assumed the stance. And so was he, he said. Unless the other was a boy. There was not likely to be any way of being sure. There were no papers scattered around—there wouldn't be. No napkins with lipstick smears. No crumpled pack of women's cigarettes. She would have picked all that up.

He threaded the maze once again. Brush heaps, sawdust streaks, footprints (large and small), but no sandwich wrapper, no beer cans, no apple cores: the little birds had eaten up all the crumbs. He did find a blue bandana caught in a bush. It had been folded into a triangle and knotted. He turned it slowly on his hands. So it really was a woman—there were no sharp folds in the fabric as if a man had folded it for a sweatband. He saw them bent to their work, reaching and withdrawing, withdrawing and reaching. If they had made love they wouldn't have left a condom lying around—if they used one, of course. He was old enough to be oriented to condoms and automatically checked the ground. No lipstick napkins. No women's cigarettes. No used Kotex. No condoms. He almost heard the breathing of their saw. Reach. Reach. Reach. He thought it would be a good idea to get back to the power line and be on his way. The day was wearing on.

He rested again at the top of the hill and then went on across a long plateau. The ferns gave way in places to blackberry thickets. Doves clapped up as he walked. They whistled off in great arcs, swinging back again as he passed on. For some time now he had been hearing the sound of a distant motor that he identified variously as a chain saw, a helicopter, an ancient lobster boat. The noise grew very loud as he was passing through a blackberry tunnel. He stopped and looked up for the helicopter. As he turned, however, he saw motorcycles bearing down on him, a great number of motorcycles in a long line. The riders were covered with mud. Only their great goggle eyes stood out from the mass of men and machines. The one in front had an enormous 115 pinned to its front. By the time he understood that they were really there, the only thing for him to do was to put his hands over his eyes and dive into the brambles.

When they had all passed and the noise was no longer a helicopter, not quite a chain saw, scarcely even a lobster boat on a foggy morning—when it was finally safe again, he still lay where he had landed. After all, climbing out of the thicket was likely to be only slightly less painful than diving in. So much for solitude.

He had finally managed to settle down in his study. His wife had gone to bed early and left him to pass out the trick-or-treat candy. She would be sleeping now, propped up, with her glasses on and her book open on her stomach. He hadn't known what to say to witches, goblins, transvestite gypsies, so he gave them handfuls of candy and told them, "Ho, ho, ho," which he knew was wrong. But they didn't seem to mind. As often as not they bungled their trick or treat anyway. Finally went out and looked up and down the street. No one. He came in and turned off the porch light.

He had barely got his papers spread on his desk when his daughter—the last child left at home—came to his door and told him that some people from his office were downstairs to see him. "Thank you," he said. She was too old to go out for trick or treat, too old even to go out defiantly, knowing she was too old. Jesus Christ, he said to himself. It was enough to have to bring the work home without having his people track him down here. Trying to look happy about the visit, he started for the stairs.

"What is it?" his wife called, half awake.

"Just some people from the office," he said.

"I won't come down," she said.

"No," he said. "Don't bother." All he needed was to have her simpering over them—and that was at best.

They were not any of the people he saw every day, so, although he knew them perfectly well, he was completely off balance. "I expected people from the office," he said at last.

"We said we used to work for you," they said. There were three of them, three women, and they were lined up on the sofa in the living room like—or was it unlike?—the three monkeys: See No Evil, Hear No Evil, Speak No Evil. It better be *like*. He had secretly lusted after each of them at one time or another.

"Sometimes my daughter doesn't hear so well," he said.

"We know," they said. "We have teenagers of our own."

"How long has it been?" he said.

"Fifteen years," they said.

"Yes," he said, "you passed the job from hand to hand."

"We passed you from hand to hand," one of them said. Her name was Emily.

He could not help saying "Ah," but did not linger over it. "To what do I owe this delightful surprise?" he said. He had fallen into a bantering tone which he was afraid was very much worse than a simper.

"Do you remember meeting me on the Mall a couple of weeks ago?" Emily said.

He had repressed the memory completely, but of course he said, "Yes." He had long ago decided that it was no good to think of her—of the other women—any other women.

"Do you remember what you said to me?"

"I'm afraid not," he said. Whatever it was it surely wasn't what he had wanted to say, what he resolved again and again he would say next time they met.

"You said very plaintively that you regretted having the children all grown up, because now no one would go out at Halloween and bring you back candy corn."

"Of course I must have said that," he said. "It's one of the great regrets of my life and particularly painful at this time of year."

"So we brought you these," they said. The other two faded in briefly from their Cheshire Cat limbo. They all held out little packets of candy corn wrapped in kitchen plastic.

He said, "My word," which expressed a number of genuine emotions, and gravely opened Emily's packet and sampled the corn before he passed it to the others. They each took a single piece.

"We had a pact in those days," Emily said, "that one of us would seduce you."

"What a nice idea," he said.

"We thought so," they said.

"We thought it would be good for you," they said.

"Whatever for?" he said.

"You seemed very unhappy," they said.

"So much for my masquerade," he said. "And that was fifteen years ago. Would you like another candy corn?" he said.

"No thank you," they said.

"And now you're all grown up and married and divorced and raising families and about to become Ph.D.s or something."

"Mostly or something," Emily said. "Nobody wants to hire Ph.D.s any more."

"Are you sure you don't want any more candy corn?" He reached toward them.

"We thought you might like to come out for a beer," Emily said.

"Lovely," he said. And he never went back.

It really wasn't bad there at the bottom of the thicket. He lay on his back and watched a great wedge of geese overtake him and pass on along the power line, very high, baying like hounds in a tapestry. He could see them for a long time. Then, using his pack, first as a launching pad and then as a buffer, he made his way back to the path. He added scratches to the scratches he already had, but only a few. He had got out of it remarkably well. No really serious gouges.

Red slashes on the backs of his hands. A stinging earlobe. It could have been much worse.

Now the sun was down behind the trees. He would have to press on to find a road and some place to stay. Perhaps a motel where he could shower and lie in a clean bed and turn his glance inward to see if any insight had secretly arrived during the day, or waking in the morning to find some message: Emily will be another thirty-year mistake—or not—if any man is allowed (or forced to endure) two thirty-year mistakes in one life.

The hill ahead was very steep. He could see two bands of gray rock, one above the other rising out of the tiers of trees. That could be very sticky. He wasn't a rock climber and had no desire to begin now. To the left of the right-of-way, exactly at the crest of the hill, great dazzling flashes of light told him of a house. He could get information. Perhaps even lodging: the farmer's daughter, the sailor's wife, the frenzied widow, the languishing girl. The wicked witch. A load of rock salt up his ass. Or all of the above.

The climb was not so difficult as he had feared. The rock faces were badly eroded, and he was able, after a little searching, to find deep crevices full of—was it scree?—that he could scramble up on his hands and knees, not, however, without fearing more than once that he might fall back and gouge—smash—crush, even, under an avalanche of dislodged stone. Only when he had scrambled over the top of the second band of rock did he ask himself where the motor-cycles went. There must have been another way. Well, their way was not his way. He liked that.

He walked around the house as if it were a gingerbread house in the forest. It was not quite new but was somehow unfinished. The shingles were weathered but scaffolding was still in place on all sides. Piles of dirt from the foundation lay about untouched. A plank walkway led up to the front door over aborted stone steps. The weeds in the yard were untrampled. No path or drive led to the house from any side. He was not without theories but he was baffled:

the owner had run out of money
the owner had died
the heirs disputed the will

there was no clear title to the land
the woman for whom the house was intended died
there was no right-of-way to the house
the woman ran off with someone else
there was no water
the woman wouldn't have him

Beyond the house the land dropped steeply down again and rose at once—but not so high and not so steep—to another crest. He sighed and hesitated. In the silence he could hear trucks on a hidden highway, probably beyond the next hill. The valley was so narrow that the power line sprang in one great sweep from hilltop to hilltop. Light caught the wires brilliantly. They were like streaks of fire, like neon tubes. A single bird sat on a wire midway over the abyss. Probably a dove, but he idly turned his glasses on it and saw the mask and red back of a sparrow hawk. He was pleased and began to sink down into the shadows.

At the bottom he saw, not far from the footpath, a small pond largely choked with weeds and rushes. Birds called softly to each other but he could see none of them. He advanced stealthily, pausing, looking about him. Very far above him now, the hawk still watched, the wires flamed. He felt the ooze of the pond's edge beneath his boots, and with a wild thrashing of wings a great black duck sprang up at his feet and curved away over the water.

What Rough Beast?

Through brush and tall grass along the overgrown road that led to
the fallen bridge, the Beast was making its way to the water. The
light under the eaves of the forest where the Beast moved was not
good, although the river itself was already luminous. Mason stood
very still, no longer shivering but beginning, perhaps, to tremble.

He had finally given up the illusion that he might sleep again, and
as the light began to grow, he slid out of his sleeping bag and stood
up in the middle of the tent. He was no colder now than he had been
for the last hour, so he might as well have got up and moved about to
warm himself. He wouldn't have waked anyone. He never did.
Neither the children around him, nor the women in their tent
nearby. Laughing, they always said he must be the quietest zipper in
the whole North Country. The children had slid down into their bags
and disappeared. They were simply mounds, cocoons, bundles as if
they had been caught overnight by giant spiders and left to ripen in
the web of their sleep. Dressing, he stood carefully on one leg and
then the other, like a solemn heron teetering in the shallows.

There was a great blue heron at the sandbar when Mason came
down to the river, half asleep, incautious, fighting his shoulders and
his back. He stepped out of the shadow of the trees onto the concrete
abutment of the vanished bridge. The river was smoking all along
the reach. He was looking toward the beaver house, but out of the
corner of his eye he saw the heron move along the sandbar. He tried
not to start—it was his first great blue—and turned his head very

slowly, but the bird must have seen him at once. He had only a quick look at it—enough to catch it, though, and it was as good as in Audubon. Better. One foot lifted, head turned, *Ardea herodias*, there it stands, the edge of the print touched by a branch of balsam fir, *Abies balsamea*.

Then came the first crash in the undergrowth across the river. It had to be a crash to catch his attention. A rustle wouldn't have done. He wasn't a woodsman by any means. Another crash. Even in that uncertain light he could see the violent writhing of the bushes, and it was clear that something enormous was coming toward him, something that cared nothing for obstacles and had never felt the need of caution. He thought of running but he didn't run, and he knew he would never be sure he could have made his legs work if he had tried. The Beast was still fifty yards from the river, and the river was twenty-five yards wide at that point. It was coming very slowly— Mason thought he could feel the earth tremble under its ponderous steps—but there was no telling what it could do when it saw him. How it might run, leap, swim. My god, what was he doing there anyway?

He tried to steady himself but it was very difficult. He was more than half asleep, and even the part that was awake wasn't up to much. For two weeks he had been sleeping on the ground in his role of Master of the Children's Tent, and sleeping very badly. Not so badly as he had expected, perhaps, but close to ruinously just the same. He was up each morning at first light and usually managed by steady walking for two hours to bring himself to a reasonably acceptable state of mind and body and soul. The heron, marvelous as it was, had not waked him up. It had, if anything, deepened his sense of hallucination. He had a suspicion that he was still asleep and even wondered where and when he would wake up. He often imagined he had fallen asleep and was dreaming the years of his life. I will wake up, he would say at such times. But where? Would he be at home again? Perhaps on a summer morning with the streak of light on the wall just beginning to touch his bookcase and marking the time when he had to get up. Or would he be at college? In the army? Where did it all begin to go wrong?

He pinched himself in the traditional way and felt the pinch sharply. But he had often pinched himself in dreams and felt the pinch, so he was no further along than before.

There was a hand axe in the trunk of his car. There was a can of lighter fluid on the picnic table at the campsite lying amidst the mess made overnight by porcupines. The others would be safest in the cars. Not bad in his state of mind. But even then he saw what he was doing: assuming it had to be hostile. The Indians have to be hostile. Kong has to be hostile. Even Doctor Frankenstein's poor tender monster has to be hostile. Kill. Smash. Destroy. Get it before it gets you. But it might—it just might—be gentle. It might come out on the river bank and solemnly dance for him. It might even have come to dance for him the waking-up dance of his long dream. An ominous crash and the whole thicket surged toward the river. Birnam Wood never came to anybody for any good purpose.

So Mason wasn't running, which was good. And he was thinking, which was better. And he wasn't diving into the river to swim over and take it on, which was best of all. Not that he was used to thinking of himself as a violent man. Far from it. But he had known despair. There had been times when he walked at night through the city, visiting the scenes of muggings, hoping—well, he was never really sure what he hoped. There were times when he believed he wanted to walk onto somebody's knife or gun, and there were other times when he seemed to himself to long for a chance to take some innocent footpad apart bone by bone with his bare hands and whatever teeth he happened to have left at the time. In any case, no one ever showed, and he later came to a somewhat better state of mind. Now, at least, he didn't throw himself at the Beast's throat.

And he had done that in his time—more or less. That is, he had got down on all fours and gone at dogs, roaring for all he was worth. The effects were always gratifying. Usually the dogs ran and howled. Once he was taken into court. And once he got a great bite on his nose, which never was the same again after it was sewed up. Dogs still barked at him, though. Much more than at other people. He had noticed.

As for his bare hands, Mason knew in his saner moments that that was a joke. It must have been thirty years—more, he wasn't even twenty at the time—since he hit anybody. He liked to think about that time though. It was a good fight. Good to remember. Very even finally. There were four of them. They got him. He got one of them. He could still see that one going over on his face on the grass beside the post office in Tuscaloosa, Alabama. He could also see the boots of the rest of them as they worked him over, but he didn't feel any of it. He always thought of the fight as a draw, almost a victory at the odds. What really interested him about it, however, was that five minutes before the fight he would have laughed at the notion that he might deliberately hurt someone. After all, he had never dreamed how a knee might be used when blows were coming from all sides and he was falling down and getting up and all the blows could just as well have been hitting a tree trunk as him, except that it was so tiring, so confusing. Perhaps those nights when he walked through the city, the aura of rage around him told the footpads, who surely must have been there, more about him than he suspected himself. Perhaps he only thought he was speaking in metaphors.

Now, he waited. He began to see patches of the Beast's fur, mottled black and white. Very low to the ground for its apparent bulk. The bushes were whipping about it. The grass surged like the sea around a whale. He tried to visualize some kind of super-badger or a strange bear built like a tortoise. He had never seen anything so big, not even in a zoo, and he was seeing only part of it. The other part is worse, an echo in his head said.

There he was, doing it again. A lifetime of caution had taught him to think that way. He had had a friend once who dared to walk out on it all and go to live by himself. Within six months he was dead. It was years before Mason understood that his friend had been a very sick man and had simply gone off by himself to die as decently as he could. It wasn't then, going off by himself that killed him, but that was the way it presented itself to Mason for a very long and very terrifying time. After all, the newspapers are full of stories about men who have been found in their rooms after three days—for some reason it is always three days—in the midst of filth and empty whiskey bottles and perhaps an attempt at a message, hieroglyphics in the dust, perhaps, a scrap of paper with a few words, their light all turned in and lost forever.

And then very strangely, it all changed. He was sitting in an outhouse in Nova Scotia, peeking out through a crack in the door at the west coast of Ireland. It was the Cliffs of Moher he was seeing, to be exact. It's now, he said to himself. And he looked around to see what was now. A spider might have been now. Or a wasp. Up in a corner of the roof, a small dark mass, which he knew to be a bat, might have been now. Or the Cliffs of Moher. But something told him it was none of those. Each was interesting enough in its way, but none of them registered Inevitable when he plugged it in. Then he tried looking inside himself.

What he saw there did not displease him, but it didn't ring the bell either. At that time he was on very good terms with his liver and lights. If he chose to sit long in the outhouse, it was not that his bowels and he weren't getting on. Far from it. He had cut down so much on everything that the whole machinery was in great shape, although if he had gone on much longer he might have succeeded in phasing himself out completely. No, sitting in the outhouse was simply a device to seize a recognized privacy, quiet, an hour of meditation with nothing in front of him but the Atlantic Ocean and the Cliffs of Moher—and, of course, a stout plank door, locked, but with a good wide crack in just the right place.

This internal harmony hadn't always been the rule, however. Why—but Mason was accustomed to think of it in parables. In other words a dream from the worst of times.

"All you have to do is look," the man said in his dream. "They're always there if you'll only look." Mason had been grumbling about not having seen the geese for years, neither spring nor fall. Once he thought he heard them at night, but that might have been part of a dream—maybe even the same dream. But he looked—in his dream he looked—and he saw up into the treetops. It was as if his sight were a thing unfolding or extending like an infinite ladder. He didn't see all the way at once. Just to the treetops, where he saw a jagged stump of a limb. He knew it well because that very evening as he passed through the grove he had heard the hammering of a woodpecker—hairy, by the sound—and looking up saw it at the limb.

There was no woodpecker now, and Mason's eye went on into a black cloud, boiling and roiling in a terrifying manner, but he wasn't terrified because even in the dream he knew it was no cloud but a flock of starlings. He hadn't seen the starlings that night, but they were a common part of standing exactly where he stood in the dream and looking as he looked. And he looked through the black cloud to the very thinnest of white clouds like drapery a woman wears in a dream but no real woman ever wears—a cloud through which you sometimes see the white moon sailing. And the geese were there, a long wavering V of them. Silent in the infinite moonlight.

Mason found it odd that each time he tried for the parable of the bowels he got the dream of the geese. The dream he wanted was a very different sort of dream. He was really awake when it happened, but since such things don't come to people when they are awake, he preferred to think he had been dreaming. Actually it was just the night before the geese dream, and he dreamed he was lying awake thinking he was Christ in the Garden of Gethsemene. It is easy enough to see why he felt he had to be dreaming. He was looking at his disciples asleep around him. They were snoring and snorting in their sleep and farting and crying out. He looked them up and down, and he said, "One of you will betray me." But it wasn't so easy for him. He didn't know about Judas. He only knew one of them was out to get him. Their names weren't names like Simon or Peter or Thomas or Matthew-Mark-Luke-and-John, either. Their names were Heart and Kidneys and Liver and Lungs. And one of them had already secretly sold him out. Gall Bladder was already dead, the lousy bastard, so he wasn't the one. Mason was down on his knees in that garden sweating blood, knowing he'd had it. The next night he dreamed about the geese.

Admittedly that was from the worst of times, but it went on like that for years, a sort of low-grade grinding misery, very Russian, he fancied. Then, for no reason, the Voice spoke to him in the outhouse in Nova Scotia. He was a little slow at first but he got the message. He saw what he had been doing all his life—he had been waiting. He had been waiting to grow up. He had been waiting to get out of college. He had been waiting for the army to go away. He had been waiting for the children to grow up. He was never being. He wasn't even becoming. He was just waiting. And then when he had seen the children go off one by one—with what longing he saw them go—what was he waiting for? He was waiting for retirement. And when retirement comes, the only thing to wait for is death. Then the Voice said, It's now, and he picked up his pants and followed it. After all there are worse things than dying alone in your room, worse than trying to write a clue in the dust of the floor or tracing a word in your own blood or leaving behind no more cryptic flotsam than a welter of empty whiskey bottles.

The Beast was coming on like a tank. Nothing made any difference to it. Its back rose and fell as if it rolled over stumps and stones. It rocked. It jarred. Even the leaves whipping as it passed sounded like the bursting roar of great gears. It was getting very close to the edge of the water. Clearly it would come down beside the abutment facing him, a gentle slope, probably a ford far older than the missing bridge. Then it would have only to lift its head to see him—if it ever did bother to lift its head.

Mason knew there were a lot of beasts that didn't lift their heads for one reason or another. There were years when he himself went around studying the ground like Mammon studying the golden pavement of Heaven. Except that he didn't see any gold. He was willing to admit that going around like that kept him from stepping in an awful lot of dog shit, but then, not stepping in dog shit, although a good enough idea in itself, wasn't the kind of idea he could actually live by. Of course looking at the ground was just an excuse for not looking at girls. Especially in spring. They would leave off their coats on the first warm day, and it was like raking off the winter mulch and finding crocuses, bursting, blooming. Totally unsuspected. Well, not looking at girls wasn't an idea he could live by either, so after a while he licked the problem of not looking, and then he licked the problem of looking—unless it was that age had licked him.

It might have been age, but Mason didn't think so. He was sleeping on the ground and surviving it. He was out on the trails every day or in boats with the children. They pretended it was some kind of Wilderness Test and were always measuring themselves against hills and against currents, against time and against darkness, against thirst, against hunger, against fatigue, and, most curiously of all, against him. They could have worn him down, too, if they had only known it. But on the trails they would run around him in circles like dogs, dashing off to one side and then the other, running ahead and circling behind, climbing trees and racing up rock faces while he plugged along at the trail, and then they would be amazed when he arrived at the summit as soon as they did and a good deal less winded.

None of these children were his, incidentally. His children were all much older, all off on their own. No, these children belonged to the women. Not that the women would have accepted the idea that one human being could belong to another—barbaric notion—but the fact was that those three women were the mothers of these seven children. By the same token, none of the women belonged to him either, although in a deep and hidden part of himself a murmured dialogue went on in a very old-fashioned vocabulary about one of them. He knew better than to let it surface, however.

What he did let surface was mainly endurance. There would be no point in asking him the difference between enduring and waiting. He wouldn't be able to answer that question. He had thought a lot about it at one time and another, but he couldn't answer it. He only knew that after the Voice spoke to him in the Nova Scotia outhouse everything was changed. It really was now, sharp and bright, as if he had been adjusting his binoculars and suddenly hit on the right focus. Even enduring was now. After all, she was there. For days on end she might say nothing more personal than "More soup?" "We need water." "We'll take the coast road tomorrow." But it was enough. It had to be. She was the only experienced camper and had the whole expedition on her back. He could look after himself—and a little more—so that was how it was: Master of the Children's Tent, Driver of what amounted to the Detention Car. You couldn't expect kids to endure, not quietly, anyway, not like an expert. It was no more than he had bargained for.

The original plan had been for Mason and her to take her kids and go camping on his vacation at the end of August. They talked it over and then consulted with friends. The friends wanted to go along. And then more friends. And then some dropped out. Others joined. It wasn't until it was too late to back out—if he had wanted to—that Mason realized that all the couples had decided not to go and that he was the only adult male still planning to make the trip.

What Mason couldn't understand was why the women had continued to encourage him to go with them. They were none of them the kind to feel the value of a symbolic male. Very far from it indeed. They had their lives well under control. They had their houses, their children, their careers, and they had among them—yes—two brown belts in Karate, one very large cup for pistol marksmanship, one membership in a carpenters' union, one law degree, one certificate from a school of automobile maintenance, and various other trophies that used to depress the hell out of him sometimes as he totted them up about 4:30 or so in the morning while he was lying there cold and sore and perhaps trying to sustain himself with the illusion that he could pick her breathing out of all the others. But, he knew, it doesn't have to be always 4:30 in the dark night of the soul. Not by any means. Certainly not after you have seen the shadow of your outhouse stretch away toward the shining Cliffs of Moher on a brilliant summer's day.

The cover was very thin near the river, but the Beast sank into it as it came on. Leaves and grass continued to whip about it. It was coming, hiding behind every blade of grass, smashing each bush beneath it, hiding from everything, caring for nothing. Mason had heard of great lions hidden in a inch of grass. He had heard of the wild crash of elephants through forests. He had heard of ghost bulls that charged through men and left them alive—if their hearts could stand it. His heart was pounding but not with terror. He was all right and he knew it. He was up on the balls of his feet ready to jump ten feet in any direction—any.

"My dear," he said, allowing himself in extremity a scrap of the forbidden dialect, "my dear." He was absolutely focused on the Beast, but he was talking to her as well, each image as clear and as whole as each of his children getting all of his love. But that was about all there was to say—that is, it was what he had to say but he mustn't say it. He had to keep quiet so she could speak. He had to refrain from moving so she could move. He had to shower her with options and never ask himself if each one for her closed out one of his own. The most discouraging thing about revolutions, he found, was that they tend simply to reverse the roles of victim and persecutor, no matter how noble the intention. It was all very difficult. To be sure of avoiding both roles. The difficulty was endless. But in moments of greatest clarity he knew it was worth it. Joy, pure joy, for whole seconds at a time.

He saw every blade of grass at the water's edge, every leaf, every hair on the back of the Beast, hidden for the last blink of an eye before it stepped out into the river.

"Beast," he said, "oh, dear Beast, oh, my dear."